SERGEANT
GRINGO

Also by Jack Cummings
Dead Man's Medal

SERGEANT GRINGO

by Jack Cummings

Walker and Company
New York

B-2

AUTHOR'S NOTE

The characters in this novel, except for certain historical figures, are fictitious, as is the story of the imaginary U.S. cavalry unit that joins General Pershing's punitive expedition into Mexico.

First published in the United States of America in 1984 by the Walker Publishing Company, Inc.

Published simultaneously in Canada by John Wiley & Sons Canada, Limited, Rexdale, Ontario.

Library of Congress Cataloging in Publication Data

Cummings, Jack, 1940–
    Sergeant Gringo.

    I. Title.
PS3553.U444S4   1984   813'.54   84-15290
ISBN 0-8027-4044-8

Printed in the United States of America

10 9 8 7 6 5 4 3 2 1

PROLOGUE

THE town of Gunlock wasn't much. It lay three miles north of the Mexican border, a jumble of cracked adobes and sun-blistered wood shacks. In slightly better shape were a false-front general store, a two-story hotel, and the mudbrick Commercial Bank.

A dirt road came up from the border, split the town in half, and disappeared into an empty part of New Mexico. Another dirt road, running east to west, divided the town alongside the tracks of the El Paso & Southwestern Railroad and was called Main Street.

Below the tracks, in the southeast quadrant thus formed, was the cavalry post, Camp Liggett. The camp was made up of a guard shack, stables and corrals, and tent barracks. There was a raw-board headquarters structure with a porch. This contained the office of the commanding officer, who was Major Everett Holcomb. In his command Major Holcomb had two troops of the 12th Cavalry, a total of 7 officers and 130 enlisted men.

The cavalry was there to protect American soil from the Mexicans, in case the Revolution spilled across the border.

The town was there to accept the Mexican cattle sometimes driven up from the great, sprawling haciendas of Chihuahua.

In the earlier years of the Revolution, Pancho Villa used to drive the cattle up, after he'd confiscated them from the wealthy *hacendados*. That was the way he paid for the guns and ammunition supplied by the Americans.

Now, in March of 1916, in the sixth year of the Revolution, things were going badly for Villa, and he was enraged by the Americans. He did not deal with them anymore, and his army had dwindled to a few guerrilla bands under roving leaders.

The cattle, when they came at all, were driven up once again by the peons of the *hacendados* and were escorted by the federal troops of Carranza.

Villa was now raging at the Americans because their politicians had double-crossed him. The American politicians had switched to backing Carranza, who claimed he was the official Mexican government.

What really made Villa rabid was that the Americans had let Carranza move his federal troops on United States rails to reinforce Agua Prieta, on the Sonora-Arizona border. That was in November. Villa didn't know about the reinforcements, and when he attacked Agua Prieta, more than two thousand of his men were slaughtered. He was forced to retreat across the Sierra Madre into Chihuahua, and his once-great Division of the North fell apart.

What happened at Agua Prieta was something that those of Villa's men who'd survived would not forget in a hurry.

CHAPTER 1

SERGEANT Matt Dunn was in the two-room shack he had rented for his quarters a block up the street from the camp. One room was kitchen and sitting room. The other was the bedroom. It was early afternoon and Matt was off duty and he was making love to Molly, his bride of less than a month.

The sharp rap at the door came at a bad moment. And after a wait the rap got impatient and increasingly insistent.

"Goddamit!" Matt said.

Molly began to giggle.

Matt pulled loose from her embrace, got out of bed, and pulled on his pants. He went out through the other room to the front door and jerked it open. One of Major Holcomb's orderlies stood there. It was Corporal Lansing, and he was smirking as he saw that Matt was mostly undressed.

"Well?" Matt said.

"Sorry, Sergeant. But Major Holcomb wants you to report to him—on the double."

"All right," Matt said. The March air was crisp and cold on Matt's bare chest. Lansing kept trying to see inside toward the bedroom, but Matt slammed the door in his face.

He went back into the bedroom. He swore again.

Molly sat up, holding the covers to her so that they barely hid her breasts. Her skin had a rare creaminess that contrasted beautifully with her Irish auburn hair and her green eyes.

Matt's face softened. She smiled back, serene and satisfied.

"I've got to report," he said, pulling on his shirt.

"It's just as well," Molly said. "I've got to get back to the dress shop."

"Less than a year to go," he said, "and my enlistment will be up. No more interruptions then." He went over to the bed, leaned down, and kissed her. The heat surged in him again.

"I can hardly wait," she said. "I'm jealous of the army, Matt."

"*Hasta luego, querida.*"

"You know I don't understand Spanish," she said.

He started down the road toward the camp and suddenly there was a Mexican at his elbow. "*Hola,* Nacho," Matt said.

Nacho Arriola had smooth skin and gray hair and black, old-looking eyes. He could have been forty or he could have been sixty. All Matt knew about him was that he sometimes worked across the border for an American-owned cattle company. When work for the company was slack, he lived in a shack on the edge of Gunlock. He wore American-style clothes—worn Levi's, flannel shirt—but his cowboy hat was straw. And he wore huarache sandals instead of boots. Matt had met him occasionally in a bar near the Mexican edge of the town.

"*Qué pasa, amigo?*" Matt said. "*Hay de nuevo?* There is something new?"

"*Sí, sargento,*" Nacho said. "I have news, I think." He hesitated, then went on in English: "At first I wasn't going to tell you. But I am American-born, you know. That is why I tell you this. A Mexican from the other side, he maybe wouldn't tell you. But I was born in El Paso. I am an American citizen."

"I know," Matt said. "You told me one time when we were drinking beer together."

"*Sí*, I remember. And you told me about the time you were in Villa's Gringo Legion." He paused. "I tell you now what I hear. You can believe it or not. But I heard it from a cousin and, me, I believe it."

"*Dígame, amigo*," Matt said. "Tell me, if I should know."

"My cousin, he works where I do on the other side, but he has steady work there. He lives on the rancho. And two days ago he was out hunting stray cattle and he saw a big encampment of men with rifles and *bandoleras*. And horses too, of course. He thinks maybe they are Villistas. Certainly they are not Carrancistas — they do not wear *federale* uniforms."

"How many men?"

"A hundred, maybe. Maybe two. My cousin, he did not wait around to count. He came to town this morning and he told me."

"You think they are Villa's men?"

"*Creo qué sí.* I believe yes."

"Your cousin did not see Villa?"

"No. He would know Villa if he saw him. Everybody has seen at least a picture of Villa."

"Why does he think they were Villistas?"

"Who else, Mateo? Maybe they were only bandits. Still, I thought the cavalry should know. So I tell you, my sergeant friend."

"Many thanks, Nacho," Matt said. "I will take this word to the major."

"At first I wasn't going to tell you," Nacho said. "It is hard for those like me. My blood is Mexican. Poor Mexican. And Villa has done much for poor Mexicans in Chihuahua."

"I understand," Matt said.

"But I was born in El Paso, so I am an American."

"I understand," Matt said again.

"So that is why I tell you," Nacho said.

Matt stopped on the headquarters porch to stomp the

dust from his cavalry boots. He opened the door and went in.

Corporal Lansing got up from a crude table littered with papers and went to the C.O.'s doorway. He said, "Sergeant Dunn is here, sir."

Matt heard the major grunt. The corporal jerked his head for Matt to enter.

Matt stepped in and stood at attention. "Sergeant Dunn, sir."

Major Holcomb was reading; he did not raise his eyes.

Matt waited impassively, masking his dislike of the major. Holcomb had assumed command of the detachment only two weeks before and he wasn't the kind of C.O. that soldiers were fond of. Holcomb finally tossed what he had been reading onto his desk — a copy of that month's *Cavalry Journal.*

Holcomb looked up at him, his small, wiry frame as erect in his chair as it was in his saddle. He was lean, dried out, and looked as tough as whang leather. You could have seen him in civilian clothes, Matt thought, and still have guessed he was a cavalry officer. He had been one for eighteen years. He was a forty-year-old major, and Matt would have bet he was dying to make colonel.

"At ease, Sergeant."

Matt relaxed slightly.

"I called you in to get acquainted," Holcomb said. "A habit of mine. When I take over a post I like to know something about the men who serve under me, and certain aspects of your own background in particular have caught my interest."

"Yes, sir."

"I understand you were married recently."

"Yes, sir."

"To a town girl."

Matt didn't like the way he put that. "My wife runs a dress shop for ladies here in Gunlock, yes, sir. But she is not a *town girl,* sir."

Holcomb's eyes slitted, but he made no issue of Matt's comment. "A soldier's life along the border being what it is today, not many noncoms are getting married."

"I've got less than a year to go on my enlistment, sir. I found a girl I love and I didn't want her to get away."

"I see. Well, a woman's a woman as far as I'm concerned. I have desires for them as strong as the next man's. But so far I've avoided the marriage trap." Holcomb broke off suddenly, frowning. "But I didn't call you in to discuss relationships with women."

"No, sir."

"It has come to my attention that you once rode with Pancho Villa. As a hired mercenary."

"I was a volunteer with him, yes, sir. When I was twenty-two years old. Quite a few Americans joined up with him at the start of the Revolution. We made up what he called his Gringo Legion."

"The man is a bandit."

"Maybe so, sir. But in the beginning, when he was fighting to overthrow the dictator Porfirio Díaz and his corruption and to help the *peónes* to live a decent life, he was something more than that. He really wanted to help his people."

"A matter of opinion," the major said. "However, this peculiar background of yours might have some value in the near future."

"In what way, sir?"

Holcomb shrugged. "Let me ask you this. In a conflict with Villa, where would your loyalty be?"

Matt was startled. It was a moment before he could speak. Then he said, "I swore my loyalty to the United States when I joined the cavalry."

"So you did, Sergeant. And don't you ever forget that. Speak Spanish, do you?"

"Yes, sir. I was about a year with Villa. I picked it up pretty well."

"Are you part Mexican?"

"No, sir. Full Irish."

"Good. I don't want any Mexicans in my command. There is another thing, Dunn. I don't approve of enlisted personnel taking on family responsibilities. It destroys their fighting effectiveness. However, in your case, the deed was done under my predecessor. But I will not allow my noncoms to live off the post. Your wife can keep her quarters, but you'll have to bunk here in the camp." The major's seamed face took on a leer. "You've been married a month. You shouldn't need your ashes hauled so often now."

"But sir—"

"That's all, Sergeant. Get your gear moved back to base. You will be quartered here again. Starting tonight. And that's an order."

Matt saluted and started to turn, then hesitated and remained standing.

Holcomb had picked up his *Cavalry Journal* again and opened it. He looked up in irritation. "Well?"

"There is something else, sir. On my way down here a Mexican I know told me something you maybe ought to hear."

"Yes?"

"He says he heard from a cousin that some of Villa's men have been seen camped just below the border."

"You don't really believe anything these local Mexicans tell you, do you, Sergeant? They love to lie to an American."

"I have no reason to think he'd lie to me, sir."

"I have," the major said. He took a paper from a drawer of his desk and held it up. "Here's a communiqué from headquarters, Southern Department of Army, Fort Sam Houston, Texas. Direct to me from Major General Funston. I won't read it to you, but the gist of it is this: *Reliable* information—notice the stress on *reliable*—has been received that Villa is planning to cross the border at El Paso and give himself up, seeking asylum from American authorities." He dropped the communiqué back on the desk. "Your former hero, it appears, is afraid of ending up before a Carranza firing squad."

Matt shook his head. "I don't believe that, sir. Villa is wild—crazy, maybe—but he is afraid of nothing. He would never give up."

"You'd believe the word of some local peon over that of General Funston?"

"With all due respect, sir, I'd believe his information over what you say is in that communication."

"Well, Sergeant, I choose to believe otherwise." Holcomb took up his *Journal* once more. "That's all, Sergeant."

When Molly came home to the shack, Matt was there to meet her. She threw her arms around his neck and pulled his face down to hers, pressing her firm, soft body against his sinewy hardness. She held tight to him like that for a long, delicious moment, her hands slipping over his shoulders to knead lovingly the rippling muscles of his back. "Matt, Matt, you have no fat," she said.

"Not likely to get any, either," he said. "Not on the grub the army feeds me."

"I can fix that," she said. "Just wait till my home cooking catches up with you."

"I don't think it will quite yet—the major's ordered me to live on the post."

She let go of him and drew back to stare at his face. "Don't joke like that," she said.

"It's not a joke. That's why he called me in this afternoon."

"But why? Why, when we're only a block from the camp? We took this place so you'd be close enough. Major Rourke agreed to it."

"Major Rourke is gone now, you know that. Holcomb is another breed of cat."

"But why, Matt? Why is he doing this?"

He shrugged. Then he said, his own anger showing, "Because he's a sonofabitch!"

"But what reason did he give?"

"Since when does a major give his reasons to a non-com?"

"I hate him!" Molly said. "I don't even know him, but I hate him!"

"Look," he said, "if you're afraid of being alone at night, you can move back uptown to the boardinghouse again."

"I'm not afraid! What's there to be afraid of? I've been alone most of my life—since I was a child, anyway. But I'm mad! Mad at that unfeeling brass bastard—"

Matt grinned suddenly. "Now, Molly. Anybody would think you had Irish in you, to judge by your temper."

"And that I have and you damned well know it."

He laughed. "Too bad the cavalry doesn't take in women. What a fighter you would make! Why, the Apaches would have given up twenty years sooner, had you been there. And the Mexicans—" He broke off sharply as a thought struck him. "No, I can't say that about the Mexicans. They have used women of their own in their fighting forces many times, at least in their irregulars. *Soldaderas,* they call them."

"I would like to meet your new major!"

"And I hope *that* never comes about. A sergeant's life under him is tough enough as it is, without you making it worse."

She smiled suddenly, then shrugged. "Well, I guess there's not much to be done about it. But can you stay for an early supper?"

"An early supper and that's all."

But he took a chance and stayed later. As it was he just got back into camp as the call for lights-out was sounding.

It was a hell of a dark night in the town, Matt was thinking. It'd be better to keep those kerosene lamps burning.

It was dark, too, where the Villistas were breaking camp after a day of resting for the night's action. There were two companies of them, each under the command of a colonel. That was the condition of Villa's army—officers who had once led regiments now commanded less than two hundred men.

They were bitter men who had survived the treachery at Agua Prieta. One of them was Captain Rodolfo Quintero, who did not command either company but had waited since November for this chance, he and a half-dozen survivors of the command he had held at Prieta.

At Prieta his men had been among the hardest hit, and though it had been no fault of his, he had never gotten another chance to lead as Villa's army nearly dissolved. This added to his hatred of the Americans and to his lust for revenge.

Quintero's blood lust was sexual too. He hoped, this night, to do more than just kill gringos. He hoped to murder and to rape. He had hungered for release through both since Prieta.

One of his men, a former corporal, said now, *"Mi capitán,* will there be women, do you think?"

"Women? Maybe," Quintero said. "But the killing is more important."

The corporal said, "I have been a long time without a woman."

"I have never had a *gringa* woman," another said. "I wonder if it is the same with them."

"It is the same, of course," the corporal said. "But it has been a long time since I had one of any kind."

Quintero thought about this. He had been a long time without a woman, too. But he said again, "The killing is more important. Do not forget that. Do not forget those coils of barbed wire we were caught on at Agua Prieta. Do not forget they were sold to the Carrancistas by the *yanquis.*"

"I will remember that," another of his half dozen said. "I lost my brother on the wire."

Quintero said, "And do not forget those electric searchlights from north of the town. *Yanqui* searchlights lit by *yanqui* power that turned the darkness of our night cover to day. That made targets of us there on the wire for the guns and the artillery of the Carrancistas. Remember—the Carrancistas did not beat us at Prieta, the *yanquis* did."

"None of us are forgetting, *mi capitán,*" the corporal said. "None of us will ever forget." He paused, then said, "Still, I would like to find a *gringa* woman there tonight— if there is time, of course. I would show her how a Mexican can use a gun."

"*Eeeayy!*" another said. "The way I am feeling now, it would not take much to explode."

Quintero did not often smile, but now he did. "Hombres," he said, "you know, you have given me something to think about."

He stood there staring into the dying embers of their camp fire, the glow casting shadows across his gaunt, aquiline features, a tall man with crossed bandoliers hung from his wide, lean shoulders. He said suddenly, "*Vámonos!* Mount up. It is time to ride."

They rode in a column of twos, stretching a quarter mile over the undulating terrain, a monstrous dark snake, rifle fangs catching glints from the stars, crawling sinuously toward the border.

Quintero and his band of survivors rode at the tail. Quintero did not like that, but it was where the colonel had ordered him to be. Well, it did not matter much, Quintero thought. Villa was through. There was no future with Villa now, or with Villa's colonels. When this night's work was over he would take his handful of men and go back to his ranch near Mapimí, in the state of Durango, and set up his own bandit fiefdom.

He had learned much from Villa. It was time now to go into business for himself. He had a reputation of sorts as a killer, because Villa had sometimes used him as an executioner of prisoners. Villa seemed fascinated by the way Quintero would go down the line shooting prisoners with his .45 revolver. Not everybody had the balls for that.

Quintero was proud of his reputation. El Matador, some of the *peónes* called him. "The Killer." His reputation would be enough to frighten a lot of people around Mapimí. In fact, if it were used right his reputation could be worth gold. Gold from the wealthy *hacendados*. Extortion, robbery—there were all kinds of fine opportunities for a man with Quintero's qualifications.

His corporal broke his train of thought. "*Mi capitán,* I do not like to be so far behind."

"*No te apures,*" Quintero said. "Do not concern yourself, hombre. There will be gringos enough to go around."

"And maybe a *gringa* or two, eh, *mi capitán?*"

Quintero did not answer him, though the corporal's words made sense; there was more than one way to satisfy a man's need for revenge.

A half mile from the sleeping town, in the dark hour before dawn, the serpentine column drew in its tail and coiled for the strike.

In the main part of the town there were only a few kerosene-lamp-lit windows to show the target. In the camp, where the squadron sentries were, there were no lights at all.

One of the sentries heard a sound and called out a challenge.

His answer was a Mexican curse and a bullet in the gut.

CHAPTER 2

THE shot brought the officer of the day, Lieutenant Darwin, out of his quarters at a dead run. He rounded a corner of the guard shack, his pistol in his hand, and smashed head-on against the horse of the raider who had shot the sentry. In the starlight Darwin saw the Mexican raise his gun. Darwin fired first and saw the man fall from his saddle.

At that moment Sergeant Matt Dunn and some of D Troop fell out of their tents, pulling pants over their underwear and carrying weapons.

Darwin said, "Two minutes to get ammo belts and boots!" He and Matt could both see the mounted shadowy forms moving up the road toward the town. Without waiting, Darwin moved out.

Matt ducked back into the barracks, grabbed his boots and belt, and caught up with the lieutenant as he reached the El Paso & Southwestern rail embankment. Matt said, "Sir, where are we heading?"

"These are some of Villa's guerrillas, I figure. If so, their prize target could be the bank at the east end of Main Street."

"What about the camp here?"

"They won't attack the camp. They'll pick the easy targets, the civilians," Darwin said. "That's my guess."

More of D Troop joined them, buckling ammo belts and swearing.

The lieutenant said to Matt, "Let's go!" and climbed over the raised railbed, then took off running between the scatter of shacks toward the center of town.

They were halfway there when they hit a strand of barbed wire in the darkness. Trooper Bentley, one of Matt's own platoon, fell over it and discharged a round from his Springfield. The flash caught the attention of the raiders on Main, and a fusillade ripped dirt up all around them.

The men of D Troop regained their footing and charged for the bank. There was an adobe portico there; they found cover behind its columns and an adjacent wall. They stayed there, shooting back at the orange stabs of flames from the raiders' weapons partway down the street.

At the camp Lieutenant Stutz of C Troop had got his own men together just after Darwin's, all of them yelling in confusion as they fumbled for clothes and weapons. Stutz ordered his men to follow and he, too, ran for the railroad tracks. But he stopped there and, using the rise of the railbed for cover, deployed his troopers to enfilade the town from the south.

Matt Dunn crouched beside Lieutenant Darwin on the bank's portico, firing at targets of opportunity, and wondered suddenly where Major Holcomb had gone.

Another thought followed, and he said to Darwin, "The major made me move back to camp tonight—but what about the officers? Hell, except for you and Lieutenant Stutz, they all got rented houses scattered around. And the major just rented the best one, way up on the north side."

"Yeah," Darwin said. He threw a pistol shot down the street. "Well, I don't run the post, Matt."

"Bad business if they're cut off by the raiders," Matt said.

"Could be." Darwin fired again.

He's taking it cool enough, Matt thought. He liked the

young lieutenant. Darwin was five years out of West Point and the same age as Matt, but he had seen no action until now. He'd been posted to one camp or another along the border during his service, but it was five years of grinding routine. Matt knew it well enough himself. Well, another year and he'd be free of the army and he'd be with Molly all the time.

Molly! God Almighty! He'd forgotten all about her.

Urgently he said, "Lieutenant, my wife is alone in our shack!"

For the first time, Darwin took his eyes off the Mexicans down the street. He gave Matt a quick, alarmed look. "You sure?"

Matt nodded. "I got to get to her, Lieutenant. I got to."

"Sure. But how, Matt? Most of the raiding force is between us and that part of town."

"I got to go, Lieutenant."

"Go ahead, Matt. Get to her somehow."

Matt thought fast. He had to get around the Mexicans. He could try to get around to the south, but he could hear firing down toward the camp and guessed at least some of the raiding party was attacking it. He glanced to the north of town, heard no firing, saw no flashes, and sprinted in that direction.

As he ran he saw the Mexicans suddenly charge up the street, ignoring the fire of Darwin and his men. They got as far as the hotel, which faced southward, then broke ranks and rushed in shooting. Matt could hear their guns blasting away.

Matt now ran west, routing himself around the rear of the hotel, and he was already past it when the thought of the guests within struck him.

There was a second, outside stairway at the hotel—the fire escape. He saw a man in a bathrobe run out on the landing at the top of it. Two raiders came up behind the man and, laughing, threw him over the rail before Matt could raise his gun. The man struck the dusty ground with the sound of a melon splitting.

Matt fired at the shadowy figures on the landing, saw one drop, and watched the other duck back through the lighted doorway.

He stood, transfixed by indecision, the urge to get to Molly pulling him away. Then he heard a woman scream inside the hotel. Matt cursed and turned toward it. He ran to the rear door and flung it open.

He did not see Lieutenant Darwin charging west on Main.

He did see down the narrow hallway between the first-floor rooms, and framed in the end of it was the desk-clerk-manager, old Uncle Bill Hansen, standing in the lobby with his hands raised high over his white mane.

A gun blasted, and Hansen doubled over and went from sight.

A raider, fisting a revolver, stepped into the hall and jerked open the first door. A woman's voice cried out desperately, "What do you want?"

Matt yelled, and when the raider turned, Matt put a bullet into him. He moved fast down the hall to the small lobby. Hansen's body lay there. He gave it a quick glance, then turned his gun as boots pounded on the hotel porch and Lieutenant Darwin burst in.

Matt almost shot him, his nerves were that tight.

"Matt!"

Matt's finger loosened on the trigger. "Goddamit! Lieutenant."

Just then a fusillade of shots came out of somewhere and struck two large drums of kerosene stored on the porch of the general store across the street. Blazing liquid flew in all directions. Within seconds the store was an inferno and flames roared up, carrying burning shingles that were blown wide and ignited the hotel roof.

The roof was burning fast, but Matt and Darwin and the

troopers on the hotel porch were not yet aware of it. They were transfixed by the sight of the blazing mercantile.

There were raiders on the hotel's second floor harassing three women and ransacking dresser drawers for loot, and they sensed the heat on the roof. They rushed for the outside stairs, one tearing at a woman's ring. He jerked it off, dislocating her finger, and laughed at her shriek of pain. Just then part of the roof collapsed and fell through the ceiling, knocking him to the floor. The woman reached into an open drawer, lifted out a derringer, and shot him dead. Her daughter cried out for help.

Below them Matt and Darwin heard the cry and wheeled outside to meet the bandits coming down the steps. Darwin, in the lead, raised his .45, triggered, and found it empty. The Mexican in front of him grinned and shoved his own pistol even with the lieutenant's chest. Matt, rounding the corner of the porch, shot the Mexican through the head.

There was a wild, close-up mix of gunfire, men fell on both sides, and then the Mexicans reached the street and joined their comrades. They all began to backtrack to the west as the burning buildings lit up the town, and Lieutenant Stutz's riflemen, enfilading from the railbed, began to knock them down.

Darwin and Matt met glances and Darwin said, "You saved my bacon, Matt. I won't forget that. But get to Molly, man."

Matt again raced west through the backyards of the buildings lining the north side of Main, paralleling the retreat of the raiders and hoping to get ahead of them.

As Matt had mentioned to Darwin, most officers of the 12th lived with wives or families in quarters scattered all over Gunlock. Among these was Major Holcomb. Like the rest, he was cut off by the raiders.

A captain, his wife and two children living on the west

edge were awakened by the first shots fired. Before they knew what was happening, there were raiders breaking in their front door. They escaped in panic out the rear windows and hid, cramped together, in the stench of their outhouse, afraid to move.

A married lieutenant lived just north of the tracks but across the north-south road from where Lieutenant Stutz had positioned his enfiladers. When the firing began, he led his wife and small daughter to hide in the surrounding brush. Moments later the squadron adjutant, Captain Lee Hill, stumbled into their hiding place. Both officers wanted to join the troops in combat but were afraid to leave the woman and child.

The Mexicans, caught in the cross fire from Darwin's men on Main Street and the enfiladers along the railbed, were now retreating fast, in scattered bunches or alone.

One of them took refuge in the clump of brush where the two officers and the females were hiding. The lieutenant and the adjutant grabbed him and choked off his cries. They were both armed with .45s, but with the Villistas around they were afraid to fire.

The lieutenant drew a pocketknife and tried to cut the Mexican's throat as he writhed and fought to get his mouth free of the adjutant's grasp. But the knife blade was dull, and the lieutenant sawed futilely with it. His wife saw this and began to whimper uncontrollably. The lieutenant, suddenly aware of the horror of it, dropped the knife and smashed in the Mexican's skull with the butt of his pistol.

Major Holcomb, who was a light sleeper, had also awakened at the sound of the first shots. He rushed out on the porch of his rented house and stood there in his long johns staring south, toward the location of the camp on the other side of the town. He stood there swearing at his damn fool decision to rent quarters so far from the post, and at his decision to ignore the warning passed on to him by Sergeant Dunn. And then he swore at Dunn for being right when he himself was wrong. This, for a moment, bothered him most of all.

And then his years of training and experience as a cavalry officer took hold and he went into action. In moments he had slipped into uniform and boots and armed himself with a pistol. He started on the double toward the north-south road leading to the camp.

Almost at once he could see that his way was blocked by the body of Mexicans moving up the same road, apparently coming from Main Street. He hesitated, then turned to his right and ran to a small house set back from the road. It was the quarters of Captain Lee Hill, the adjutant. He banged his fist against the door.

A woman's voice said, "Go away! Touch that door and I'll shoot!"

Holcomb looked over his shoulder at another bunch of Mexicans withdrawing from Main Street and coming toward him. He shouted, "Open up!"

A handgun barked inside the house and a slug ripped through the door, sending a splintered chunk of it past his ear.

"It's me, Holcomb! For God's sake, Martha! Open up!"

There was no reply, and he gritted his teeth and stepped aside so that he was clear of the door and then reached with his knuckles to pound on it again.

The gun exploded a second time and he jerked his hand away, and a panel fell out of the door and crashed to the stoop floor.

"Martha, get a grip on yourself!"

Another shot struck the lockset and the shattered door flew open. Holcomb, cursing at the hysterical woman, rushed recklessly through the doorway and jumped sideways as the gun roared a fourth time.

He saw the stab of flame and judged her position, took three fast strides, swung his open hand hard in the darkness, and was surprised when he caught her in the jaw and felt her go down, then heard her weapon strike the floor.

He bent down and gathered her in his arms and held her. Suddenly she was crying.

"Martha," he said. "It's Everett." Then: "Where's Lee?"

She stiffened in his embrace and sat up. "He—went for the camp—when the attack—my God! Everett, I'm sorry. I lost my head—I thought—"

"I know, I know," Holcomb said. He stood up and went to the open doorway, his gun in his hand. But, strangely, the Mexicans had not noticed or had ignored the shooting at the house.

"I've got to get to the camp," he said.

"Stay here with me, Everett. I'm scared."

"Lee should have stayed."

"I'd rather have you," she said in the darkness. "You know that, Everett. It's been that way ever since Fort Bliss."

"That's all behind us, Martha. I can't keep cuckolding my own adjutant." He was still at the doorway when he heard another firefight start up in the center of the town. Good! he thought, some of the bastards are still trapped.

"Don't leave me, Everett."

"Goddamit! I've got to," he said. But still he hesitated. The firing uptown was heavy now, and he debated whether he should try to assume command there or continue to the camp. It sounded as if there was shooting at the camp too, but it was more sporadic.

Suddenly he saw the flare-up as the kerosene tanks ignited and the mercantile and the hotel caught fire. He was about to move when the enfiladers opened up from the tracks and the main body of Mexicans began to pour west toward him.

He swore again. I can't leave her now, he thought. Only woman I ever gave a good goddam about, and she has to be married to another. I can't leave her here alone with those raiders headed back this way—but I've got to get to camp and muster a force to cut them off. I can't let them get away with this, either.

The adjutant's wife had gotten up and she stood beside him, clinging to his arm and staring at the Mexicans as they drew nearer. "Don't leave me alone, Everett."

"I've got to," Holcomb said.

And then he saw the figure of a trooper running from the northeast. He reacted instantly, rushing out to intercept him, and saw the man raise his gun. "I'm Major Holcomb!" he yelled. "Halt where you are, trooper!"

Matt saw the uniform and the rank insignia reflected in the light of the burning town. He stopped. "Major," he said. He was breathing hard.

Holcomb stepped closer. "Sergeant Dunn?"

"Yes, sir. Sir, I've got to get down that street ahead of those Villistas."

"Stay where you are," Holcomb said sharply. "That's an order."

"Sorry, sir." Matt began to move ahead.

"I gave you an order," Holcomb said.

Matt exploded. "Damn your order, Major! My wife is alone down that street."

"There's an officer's wife alone right here," Holcomb said. "I'm ordering you to stay here with her."

"Stay with her yourself, then," Matt said. He found himself still holding his gun pointed at the major. "Get out of my way, Major. You're wasting my time."

Holcomb was too shocked to react. And then it was too late, and Dunn was running toward his own rented quarters, racing to beat the retreating Mexicans.

As he ran Matt gave no more thought to the major. He ran off through the desert plots that held the shacks, angling toward the one where he'd left Molly.

How could he forget her this way! That's what came from five years of soldiering, he thought. Four years in the cavalry and before that a year in Villa's Gringo Legion.

He'd been in the Legion with Captain Sammie Dreben, the greatest soldier of fortune of them all, and with Captain Tracy Richardson, who was nearly as good, and with Captain Oscar Creighton, who was called the Crazy Dynamiter. He'd been there when they had taken the city of Juárez for the Revolution. And for Villa. Then it was *Viva Revolución! Viva Villa!* But not now. The Revolution had become so confused—one faction fighting another until a man couldn't get straight who or what he was fighting for. And maybe that was what had finally happened to Pancho Villa himself.

After a year of it Matt couldn't stomach the way Pancho was killing, even though he claimed to stand up for the peons, so Matt quit the Legion.

Well, dammit! he was married now, and it was time he started thinking like a married man. He ran faster, the chill air of near dawn raw in his throat. Never should have left her alone, he thought, never should have left her alone.

He saw the shack from a hundred yards away and felt relief that it wasn't burning. There was lamplight showing through a window, though, and that surprised him. And then as he neared he saw the reflection of the light glistening on the silver studdings of a Mexican saddle. And the horse tied to the post in front of the shack.

Panic increased his sprint. It made him reckless, too, and he flung himself at the door, his gun in his hand.

The door burst open and he charged across the sitting room to the other doorway.

The kerosene lamp flickered in the rush of air he caused, distorting the shadows around the bed. It took him a few seconds to see that the Mexican had Molly there, her nightgown ripped upward to bare her flesh, and that he was raping her.

The Mexican heard Matt's boots striking the floor and he twisted his head and saw him and grabbed at his six-gun hung over a chair beside the bed.

Matt was afraid to shoot, afraid of hitting Molly. He gave a strangled cry and leapt forward. The Mexican got his pistol loose from his holster and shot from where he lay, his body still coupled with Molly's.

The bullet struck Matt's skull with clubbing impact and blackness took him.

He fought his way back to consciousness, hearing the crackling of the flames, feeling the heat. He struggled to his knees and knew the shack was burning, and then he saw Molly lying still and alone on the bed, her nightgown and the bedclothes afire.

He got to his feet somehow, staggered to her, and beat at the flaming clothes with his open hands. Then, as the fire swept around them, he grabbed her up and rushed blindly for the doorway. He got through the outer room, through the outer door, and fell with her twenty paces from the shack as it went up in a roar.

The shock of the fall brought her to a moment of lucidity. Eyes still closed, her lips moved in a mask of seared flesh as he smothered her burning gown with his body. He peered close, and his horror at the sight caused him to whimper.

The loveliness of her face was gone and he could see the broken jaw where the Mexican had hit her with his gun barrel.

"Molly, Molly," he cried.

Her eyes flickered open and she knew him. "Matt," she whispered. "He told me his name. Bragging, he was." Then: "I loved you, Matt."

"Molly, oh God! Molly."

"Captain Quintero—and—he broke—the lamp—on purpose."

He echoed the name. "Quintero."

She cried out in the agony of her burns. He wanted to hold her to him, but he was afraid of hurting her more.

Her eyes found his and her temper flared one final time. "Get him for me, Matt," she said. "Don't let him get away. Kill him for me, Matt. Go—after him—now!"

Her eyes closed then and she was gone.

He was still cradling her scorched body in his arms when Lieutenant Darwin found him. The lieutenant stopped and stared at him, and at first he could not speak. He just kept looking at Matt and then at the smoldering remains of the shack and avoiding looking a second time at Molly until he thought he knew pretty much what happened.

He also thought he knew what was best for Matt at this moment.

He said, "She's dead, Matt. And we're going after those who did this to her. Come along and mount up."

Matt looked up at him and saw that daylight had come. He nodded and laid Molly down gently against the ground and stood up. He passed his hand across his face and looked blankly at the blood on it, which was pouring down from the bone-deep furrow made by Quintero's bullet, where it had creased his scalp.

She had said, "Kill him for me, Matt. *Go after him now!*"

He nodded and fell in beside Lieutenant Darwin, and they began to walk toward the camp and their horses.

CHAPTER 3

THE raiders withdrew from the town and retreated down the road toward the border, sending back sporadic fire in rearguard action.

The officers who had been trapped in town came out running for the camp. First among them was Major Holcomb. He located a bugler and ordered him to sound assembly, and the clear notes of the call went out on the dawn air seeking the scattered troopers.

Holcomb began at once to form a pursuit force from the available men of both C and D troops.

Twenty minutes after the last shots had been fired in Gunlock he led out a detail of forty troopers and three officers to try to overtake the Mexicans.

Sergeant Matt Dunn, still in a state of shock, was with them, a bloody compress showing on his forehead beneath his hat.

So was Lieutenant Darwin, riding at Matt's side during the first mile or two, speculatively eyeing his condition. Darwin, at that time, did not know of Dunn's insubordinate run-in with the major, but he did know that Dunn was going to have a permanent part in the middle of his hair.

It was not until Darwin rode forward to join the other officers that he learned from the major himself that Matt was on Holcomb's blacklist.

Holcomb looked at him as he rode up and said, "Lieutenant, when we return from this foray I want Sergeant

Dunn placed in the guardhouse. He will be charged with gross insubordination, refusal to obey the order of and cursing at his commanding officer."

"Sergeant Dunn?" Darwin said incredulously.

"Sergeant Dunn, Lieutenant."

"But Dunn was with me during the thick of it, sir. As a matter of fact, sir, he probably saved my life by shooting a raider who had a pistol aimed at my gut."

The major seemed not to hear. "I may think up other charges to bring against him before we get back," he said.

"May I ask, sir, why, under the circumstances, did you allow him to remain in this detail?"

Holcomb said, "It was more important that we get after those Mexican bastards. I would not be delayed. But when we return, you will carry out my order immediately."

"Yes, sir," Darwin said. "Might I ask what the particulars of his offenses were?"

"I ordered him to remain on guard at the quarters of Mrs. Hill, Captain Hill's wife. He refused. That reminds me—he also brandished a weapon in my direction in a threatening manner."

Darwin exchanged glances with Lieutenant Stutz, who rode beside him. Stutz raised his brows in a questioning manner but said nothing.

After a short silence Darwin said, "Sir, I believe there are strong extenuating circumstances to account for Sergeant Dunn's behavior."

"Is that a fact, Lieutenant?" Holcomb's tone was sardonic. "According to regulations there are no extenuating circumstances for the offenses he committed."

"Sir, his own wife was killed by the raiders—burned to death. I saw her body myself."

For a moment Holcomb appeared taken aback. Then he said, "At the time of his misconduct he could not have been aware of that. In his own words, he was on his way to her."

"It is unfortunate that he didn't reach her sooner," Darwin said, bitterness shading his words.

"Mister, are you blaming me for delaying him?"

"No, sir. You couldn't have known what was happening to her, of course. More likely I blame myself for keeping him at my side during the attack."

"That was the place for him," the major said. "The man is, or is supposed to be, a soldier."

"If I may say it, sir, he is a damn good one."

"That is not my opinion."

"Will you bring him before a court, sir?"

"A special court-martial could give him six months' confinement," Holcomb said. "I have that strongly in mind." He paused. "Bad time added to his remaining enlistment. That just might make a proper soldier out of him."

"But sir—"

"Enough, Lieutenant!" Holocomb was staring ahead, squinting into the glare of the morning sun. "By God! we're catching up to the raiders. See the dust over that ridge?"

"Yes, sir," Captain Walker, who was second in command, said. "But may I mention that we are now on the Mexican side of the border? We passed it some time back. Isn't that a violation of sovereign territory? The department, I believe, is specific in its policy of keeping us on our side of the line."

"I didn't see any line, Captain. All I saw was sand and sagebrush and greasewood. The line could be somewhere miles up ahead. This country all looks alike to me. Do you understand what I'm saying?"

Captain Walker hesitated, then said, "I understand, yes, sir. But for the record I want to state my own belief that we have passed it."

Holcomb shrugged. "I am not letting those bastards ride away scot-free. Understand?"

"Yes, sir."

"All right, then." Holcomb spurred his horse ahead of the others and rode there alone, erect and tall in the saddle, his eyes on the distant ridge that rose out of the bleak landscape. A logical spot for a rearguard action, he thought. I hope so. I've got to get another crack at the sons of bitches. I was responsible for the town's defense and I was taken by the ragtag bastards. There could be an army board of inquiry into possible negligence on my part.

The thought caused him to swear, loud enough for those behind him to hear.

"Major?" Captain Walker called.

"Nothing!" Holcomb said shortly. He dropped back and rode in silence for several minutes before he spoke again. Then he said, "They'll be laying for us behind that ridge."

"Quite likely," Walker said uneasily. "How many of them would you guess?"

"Who the hell can guess what they'll do? But a small force would be logical—a delaying action while the main body gains more of a lead."

"We might flank them, sir, do you think?" Lieutenant Stutz said. He gestured to where the ridge sloped away westward to the flat level of the plateau.

"Too far," Holcomb said. "By the time we got around, they'd be gone and the rest would be ten miles ahead of us."

"What, then?" Walker said.

"Pistol charge, right up the slope," the major said.

"They may have more men there than we'd guess."

Holcomb turned to stare at him. "We'll find out, won't we?"

The distance to the ridge was deceptive. They rode for an hour before they reached the beginning of the steep rise. It was several hundred yards from there to the crest.

Too damn far, Lieutenant Darwin was thinking.

"Captain Walker," the major said, "form the squadron in a single line."

"Single line, sir?"

"What else? We've got a provisional mix here, Captain —we do not have organized platoons. Form the line!"

Walker turned and gave the order and the word went down the column of fours, and the troopers in the front halted as those behind rode forward and to either side to form the line.

Major Holcomb rode up the slope a short way, then wheeled his horse and looked down on them. He was within long range of the ridge and could have taken a rifle bullet in his back. He knew this but logic told him the Mexicans would hold their fire, hoping to surprise the squadron.

"Draw pistols!" he commanded.

The troopers tugged loose their automatic .45s from their flap holsters and sat hunched forward and tense.

Holcomb wheeled his mount again and faced the ridge. Without looking back, he took off his hat, waved it forward, drove his spurs hard into his horse's flanks, and sent it running up the long slope.

Too goddam far, Lieutenant Darwin thought again. But he followed. One thing about the bastard, he was out there in front. You couldn't fault him for lack of guts.

They made the first two hundred yards and still no fire came from the top. They must have plenty of rifles waiting for us, Darwin thought, to hold fire this long. They must be waiting to cut us down point-blank. The horses were beginning to blow. It was too far for a charge. How the hell could you run the horses that far uphill and have anything left when you reached the top? Still, the major didn't have much choice. He couldn't walk them into the fire, either. Darwin was glad it wasn't his decision to make.

Another couple of hundred yards and a horse at the right end of the line stumbled and went down, throwing its rider. Darwin cursed, felt his own mount foundering, and knew that he would reach the top at no more than a walk. And the goddam Villistas still held their fire.

They must have their whole goddam force waiting to blast us.

They were fifty yards from the top now, more or less, the line straggling in loops as the weaker mounts fell back. Darwin looked once for Sergeant Dunn and saw him up even with him, halfway down the line to his left.

The major held his lead, never looking back. Hell, Darwin thought, we could turn tail and run and the gutty bastard would finish the charge alone. He gritted his teeth and drove his spurs in and sent his trembling horse after Holcomb's.

He was still trailing by fifteen yards when the major stormed the redoubt alone. *And still there was no fire.*

What the hell? Darwin saw the major halt on the skyline and sit his saddle while his horse sucked in great gasps of air.

The goddam fool! Darwin eased up and halted below the ridge top so he wouldn't be a sitting duck for any rifle waiting below. The line faltered to a halt behind him.

He called up. "What is it, sir?" But he knew the answer. There was no rear guard there. Old Guts-for-brains had led a classic charge on nothing at all.

He had done one thing, though. He had destroyed the horses.

The major turned slowly and looked down at Darwin. There was no expression on his tough, weathered face. His eyes met Darwin's, then flicked to the halted line of troopers. He called down in a steady voice, "Lieutenant, order the troops to dismount and lead."

"They are already dismounting, sir. But lead where? You'd best get off that skyline, sir, if I may say it."

"There are no raiders here, Lieutenant," the major said. His voice was flat and wondering.

"Yes, sir," Darwin said. "But you'd best get down, sir, don't you think?"

Holcomb dismounted and led his own mount slowly down to Darwin's side. Captain Walker and Lieutenant Stutz joined them.

"Gentlemen," Holcomb said, "here we have an example of damn poor tactics."

"You couldn't have known, of course, sir," Stutz said.

"Me? Goddamit, Stutz, I'm not referring to our assault. I'm referring to the Mexicans—they had a perfect position for a delaying action and they didn't have the brains to take advantage of it."

For a moment Darwin stared into Holcomb's face to see if he was joking. The major's expression was composed and serious.

"This points up what I've always maintained," Holcomb said. "That if we ever get a chance to go into Mexico after those bandits, we'll whip their asses so quick they won't know what hit them."

The officers looked at one another. Nobody spoke for a short moment, then Captain Walker said, "Might I mention again, sir, that we *are* in Mexico?"

"What is that supposed to mean?"

"Nothing, sir. I just thought that this would be a good time to turn back. The horses are in no condition for more action and—"

Holcomb glared at him. "Captain, *I'll* say when we turn back. I still haven't seen any border monuments. Give the horses a fifteen-minute breather and we're taking up the pursuit."

"But sir—"

"Captain, did you hear me?"

"Yes, sir."

"Pass the word to the men. Fifteen minutes and we mount up."

"Yes, sir."

Darwin sought out Matt Dunn. Dunn stared at him but said nothing. "Are you all right, Matt?"

Dunn nodded.

"Damn fool charge," the lieutenant said. "All for nothing."

Dunn said, "We're going on, though, aren't we?"

"Yes, dammit!"

"Good," Dunn said.

Darwin looked at him closely. Looking at Dunn's face was like looking at a cadaver's. "You want to go on, Matt?"

Dunn looked at him as if the question did not make sense. "I got to go on," he said. "One of them killed Molly."

Holcomb said to Walker, "We're moving out. Give the order to lead. At the top we'll remount."

The troopers tugged at unwilling horses and began the short ascent to the ridge. Seeing nothing there as they swung into their saddles, some of them grumbled in voices low so the officers wouldn't hear.

"Jeezcris! what we going to do if we do catch up with them *now?*"

"How the hell could we catch them?"

"You got a point there."

"But just suppose we *did* catch up with them?"

"Major'll know what to do." The words were said in sarcasm.

"Yeah," Trooper Novak said. "Just once I'd like to follow the lead of somebody smarter than me."

"Get down and follow your horse, then."

In a column of fours they began the descent of the long, empty slope on the other side. At the foot of the slope they could see a broad growth of thick chaparral. They could see where the trail taken by the Mexicans disappeared into growth as high as a horse's withers.

Darwin was still with Dunn, and now he said, "I don't like any of this," and forced his mount forward to where the major and Walker and Stutz were riding point.

Something didn't smell right to him.

The barrage cut loose just as he reached the others.

It came from the fringe chaparral. Captain Walker jerked in his saddle and grabbed his right shoulder with his left hand, still clutching his reins. The jerk on the bit caused his horse to pivot sharply. The troopers behind him saw him turn and took it as a move toward withdrawal, and some wheeled around to retreat.

The major yelled, "Halt! Stop those men!"

Darwin called an order, just as one fleeing trooper was shot out of his saddle and the mount of another went down, pinning its rider's leg. The others stopped, hearing the order.

Holcomb yelled, "Get off the slope! Come on, come on!" and drove straight into the fire coming from the chaparral.

There wasn't much choice, Darwin thought. A long stretch of no cover behind them. Fifty yards to cover ahead—if half of Villa's army wasn't lying there waiting for them.

They followed Holcomb again, Walker letting go of his shoulder to fumble for his pistol with his half-useless right hand.

One of the grumbling troopers swore. "Here we go again." He kicked at his horse to urge it forward and a bullet hit the horse in its chest, and it sank beneath him, the trooper leaping free.

They charged into the brush, firing blindly, no targets seen.

Once in, Holcomb shouted, "Dismount and take cover!"

The order was superfluous. No trooper was going to sit his saddle with his head sticking up above the brush to be shot off.

They waited under cover, hearing nothing but the heavy breathing of the horses at first. Then, as that lessened, they could hear the drum of hooves running on the trail away from them.

"There was the rear guard, Major," Captain Walker said bitterly. He was holding his shoulder again, pressing a wadded-up neckerchief against his wound to stanch the flow of blood.

"Should have been up on the ridge," Holcomb said. "Damn bandits don't know the rules of warfare, how can they fight by them?"

A troop sergeant came up and spoke to Walker. "We've got three wounded, sir, counting one with a busted leg. He can probably still ride, though, but it's going to hurt him like hell. Another one lost part of his ear and it's bleeding like a faucet. The third one, Private Novak, is gut shot. We got to rig a litter for him." He added, "With your permission, sir."

Holcomb seemed to be only half listening. He said, "How bad is he hurt?"

"Novak, sir? I said he's gut shot."

"Major," Walker said, "we've got to go back."

"Stinking raiders!" Holcomb said. "All right, prepare to withdraw." Then, as the officers turned away, he called, "Darwin, I want a head count here—some more wounded might have dropped off in this brush."

"Yes, sir. I'll see to it."

"Fall in!" The major sat his saddle, looking expressionlessly at the troops as they formed a column on the open slope. There was a litter made of saddle blankets slung between two horses. Private Novak, or what was left of him, was in the litter. He was unconscious, and blood and other liquids were dripping out of his body and through the blankets and staining the dry earth below.

Darwin came up leading his horse. He seemed reluctant to speak.

"Well, Lieutenant?"

"All accounted for, sir. Except one. Sergeant Dunn of my company is missing."

"Dunn!"

"Yes, sir. We've searched everywhere for him."

"Was he hit?"

Darwin hesitated. "I don't believe so, sir. Nobody who was near him seems to think so."

Holcomb stared at Darwin. "The man has deserted, then," he said.

"No, sir. Sergeant Dunn wouldn't desert, sir. But he was still in shock and obsessed with going after the killer of his wife."

"He heard the order to prepare for withdrawal," Holcomb said. "If those around him heard it, he heard it."

"Possibly, sir."

"What do you mean—*possibly?*"

"As I said, sir, he was in a state of shock. He may not have understood the order."

"Stop making excuses for him, Lieutenant. The man heard the order and chose not to obey it—went off on his own. In any book that is desertion. And that's the most serious charge against him yet."

Trooper Novak died before they had gone five miles. Just before he died he spoke aloud, his voice so weak that only the troopers leading the sling horses heard him. "Goddam major," he said. "Next time I'll follow my horse."

They walked, leading the tired horses, and they swore as the blisters burned their feet and the noonday sun burned their necks. Somebody finally noticed that Novak was dead, and they halted and lowered the sling to the ground, rolled him in the blankets, lifted him across the saddle of one of the horses, and tied him there.

They went on then, horses and men moving at a grim and plodding pace. Ahead of them the major led his own mount, striding purposefully, as if he wanted to devour the miles out of Mexico.

Captain Walker, his face set against the throbbing in the torn tissues of his shoulder, looked aside at Holcomb and muttered under his breath. Now, he thought, the bastard can't get back across the border fast enough. Now he's beginning to worry about invading foreign soil. Thinking of a possible reprimand. Thinking how it could affect future consideration for promotion. Thinking whether he will be held accountable for last night's fiasco.

Not thinking about Trooper Novak. Or the trooper with the smashed leg that they'd likely have to amputate. Or even about Corporal Fiedler, with his ear shot off. Or even me.

Lieutenant Darwin walked ten paces behind Walker, thinking about Sergeant Dunn.

The poor sonofabitch, he thought. On top of losing his wife that terrible way, he's become a target of Holcomb's resentment. And now he's heading into Mexico alone, and who the hell knows what will happen to him there.

They reached the cattle road, and soon they came to the short section of barbed-wire fence on either side that marked the border.

Captain Walker, his discretion perhaps weakened by pain, could not restrain himself from calling this to the major's attention. "This marks the line, Major."

Holcomb did not look at him. He continued to stare straight ahead but said irritably, "I see it. Do you think I'm blind?"

"No, sir," Walker said. "I point it out only because I believe you failed to see it earlier today."

"What would you have done?" Holcomb said angrily. "Let them ride off with impunity?" Before Walker could answer he said, "Order to mount up."

"Mount up?"

"Yes, goddamit! We're not going to straggle-ass back into that town, Captain. We're going to ride in style."

The exhausted detachment reached the camp in the early afternoon. It found civilian dispersal crews as well as troopers hard at work. They had dragged the dead raiders to the outskirts of Gunlock, doused them with kerosene, and set them ablaze. Added now to the ashen smell of the smoldering American town was the stench of roasting flesh.

The American dead were laid out at the undertaker's. Molly Dunn was among them, her disfigured face hidden under a heavy veil.

CHAPTER 4

THE dullness held him. Even when he heard the order of recall and withdrawal, Matt was only dimly aware of it; it did not touch him. He kept his horse moving through the chaparral and soon blundered back onto the trail. He heard no shooting now, just the sound of the horses moving as the handful of Villista rear guardsmen rode after the main body of the raiders.

Eventually he rode out of the chaparral and came onto a sparse and tawny plateau, gashed by ravines, that stretched on to disappear into a dusty haze. There was no sight of the Villistas.

In the middle of the afternoon the horse ground to a halt and stood with legs trembling, and he had the sense finally to get down and ease its burden. He removed the saddle, poured water from his canteen into his campaign hat, and held it so the horse could drink.

Then he sat in the scant shade of a creosote bush and stared into the distance. He saw Molly's face as it had been before it was burned, saw her lively, warm smile and the loving in her green eyes, and he sobbed her name and beat his fist against the earth.

The horse could not go on. Matt hobbled it in an area of scattered bunchgrass while he ate a tin of rations, and then dozed off.

A couple of hours later he resaddled and walked until dark, leading the horse. He made a dry camp then, sharing his water with the horse again. He could find no more forage.

He awoke in the cold of dawn. Again he put the saddle on the horse and led it south.

The night had been freezing, but now the sun rose in a brassy sky and the air shimmered above the arroyo-slashed desert. There was no water left for the horse, and its breathing had become labored.

His own thirst grew, and he emptied the little left in his canteen. His feet began to burn in his cavalry boots, and his calves cramped as the salt sweated from his body.

Matt had lost his alertness; his senses were blunted by the endless plodding and by the grief that welled up in his throat again and again as thoughts of Molly came back to him. Once he heard himself call out to her and he felt the tears running down his leathery jowls.

He was surprised when they closed in. At first he stared without comprehension. Then suddenly his awareness snapped back and his anger flared at having been so easily taken.

They were Quintero and his men. Six of them.

He knew the leader was Quintero, although he did not know how he knew, for he had seen the man's face only that one time in the flickering shadows with Molly.

Quintero had a revolver pointed at him. *"Con los dedos—deja caer la pistola!"* he said.

With his fingertips Matt tugged his pistol from its flap holster and let it fall.

"Good," Quintero said, "you understand Spanish."

Matt stared at him, saying nothing.

"You were looking for us?" Quintero said. "Very foolish, sergeant gringo. To come alone was a crazy thing. Too bad we waited again, eh? To see if any more *yanqui* fools would fall into another trap."

Still Matt said nothing.

"You came because of what happened at Gunlock, no?

Well, a soldier's life is a hard one. You, *sargento,* should know that. We deal in death. Death is our business."

"Not the death of women," Matt said.

Quintero stared at the caked blood on Matt's skull where his bullet had creased it. "The woman died?"

"My woman," Matt said.

Quintero's black eyes stared into Matt's.

"She burned to death in the fire you started in our house."

Quintero was silent. Then he said, "I did not intend it to be that way—not in the beginning. One thing led to another. Your *gringa* fought against my love and that was bad. Then you interrupted. I thought I killed you and she did, too, I think. She went crazy and tore at my eyes and I hit her with my gun. The lamp which caused the fire, maybe it was an accident, maybe not. But she enraged me—you understand?"

"No."

"Well, it is the truth. Quintero does not kill women, not intentionally. I kill men. I make love to women. That is what I was doing to your woman. Making love."

"Making rape."

"There is a difference?"

"There is a difference," Matt said. "And she is dead."

Quintero said, "None of this would have happened if you gringos had not betrayed us at Agua Prieta. Why did you turn against Pancho Villa?"

"I did not turn against him," Matt said. "The politicos of my country turned against him."

"You speak Spanish well."

"I fought for Villa in the beginning. I fought for him at the first Juárez."

"A gringo legionnaire, then? But now you are on the other side."

"Not by choice."

"To me, you are a traitor like that *hideputa,* that son-of-a-whore, General Orozco. He fought with Villa, too, at the first Juárez."

"I remember Orozco."

"Did you know the whore's son was killed in December? Yes? What irony! Shot to death for stealing horses. At Ojinaga—and by Texas rangers!"

"I am not Orozco."

"No. Of course not. You are only a traitorous gringo *legionario.*" Quintero studied Matt's hard face. "Well, then, *sargento gringo,* you came seeking *venganza,* eh? Vengeance. I understand that. I seek vengeance myself."

Matt stared up at him.

"So because of all this, I will have to kill you."

Matt bent to grab at his dropped pistol.

Quintero's gun blasted. Matt's pistol leaped from the touch of his fingers. Pebbles stung his hands.

"Not that way! It is too easy. So you are raging. Well, I and my men are raging, too. Did you hear about Agua Prieta, *yanqui?* And last night your soldiers killed many of our *compañeros.* I and my men can use some *venganza* ourselves."

Matt said, "Let us settle this like men. You and I in a *mano a mano.* Both armed."

Quintero showed his teeth. "A hand-to-hand? A gun duel? Why should I take the chance? There is nothing to gain for me. Nobody to witness my victory except my own men—and who would believe *them?*"

His men sat on their horses and listened.

One of them, as tall and gaunt as Quintero but of slimmer build, said, "Can we play the game, *mi capitán?*"

"*Cómo no?* Why not?" Quintero said. "Tie his ankles, Flaco."

Flaco and three of the others got down and rushed to grab Matt. Matt hit Flaco as he came in, his right fist flush on the jaw, and Flaco went down as if he were shot.

The other three caught his arms as he tried to lash out.

They threw him to the ground and pinned him. The third pulled a piggin' string from his pocket and whipped it around Matt's ankles with the dexterity of a charro.

Quintero reached behind his cantle and took a wooden picket from a saddlebag. "Stake him down," he said.

The charro looked around and found a heavy rock to use for pounding. He drove the stake into the sun-baked ground. He pulled at the stake then, testing it. "Solid," he said.

"Tie the *yanqui* to it."

The charro brought out another thong and did so.

"All right, hombres," Quintero said. "You know the game."

His men, all grinning, got on their horses and fell into a line thirty yards away. Quintero rode to one side to watch.

Matt looked at him and yelled, *"Cobarde!* Coward! Would you not face a gringo man to man?"

Quintero shrugged. "Why, when there is nobody to watch? My men will enjoy this more than a *mano a mano."*

Flaco lisped through his battered mouth, "Now, *mi capitán?"*

"Now, Flaco."

Flaco spurred his horse from the others and galloped straight toward where Matt now stood staked fast to the ground.

Matt tensed, braced himself for the shock, and then at the last second Flaco swerved to the left and brought his right hand around fisting a revolver and smashed its barrel across his face.

The blow took Matt on the cheekbone, and he felt the bone crack. It knocked him off balance, and he tripped over his tied ankles. He went down hard, landing flat on his back, his head bouncing off the earth, the wind knocked out of his lungs.

"Olé!" Quintero shouted. And laughed.

Matt heard the next rider coming and struggled to get up.

He was only halfway erect and the rider misjudged, and his knee struck Matt's shoulder. It spun Matt around and knocked him flat again. Pain shot through his twisted ankles as the piggin' string tightened on the picket. Something gave, and he thought at first that a bone had snapped. The rider pivoted beyond him and came racing back by, cursing the pain of his bruised knee.

Next up was the charro who had tied his feet, spurring a sorrel gelding. Rage took hold of Matt, a wild, hate-filled anger. He eyed the horseman racing toward him and an animal growl came from his throat. He waited in an awkward crouch, his legs ready to spring.

The sorrel shied and struck Matt's hip, and Matt clawed at the stirrup and locked his grip on it. There was a terrible tug on his legs, the stake pulled loose, and suddenly he was being dragged along.

The sorrel jumped sidewise and threw the charro, but Matt hung on to the flailing stirrup. The horse broke into a run, trying to shed the dragging burden. It plunged blindly into a thick stand of high greasewood. Branches lashed across Matt's face. The piggin' string around his ankles caught on something, cut deep into his flesh, and snapped, and his legs were free.

The horse halted. Matt pulled himself to his feet, grabbed at the reins and horn, and heaved himself up into the saddle. The sorrel, still spooked, began to pitch. It crashed through the overgrowth and came out on the edge of a deep arroyo.

Behind him Matt could hear shouting and horses moving and cursing in Spanish as Quintero's men fought their way through the greasewood.

He kicked his heels into the sorrel and plunged down into the arroyo. The sorrel made a half jump at the bottom and came up hard and went to its knees. The jar snapped Matt's teeth together.

The sorrel recovered and raced down the arroyo, somehow missing the rocks strewn in its bed. The arroyo led to a wide dry river. Matt turned south at its near edge, hugging the bank, fighting an impulse to cross the river in order to get distance from Quintero. Out there he would be an open target. Here there was dense scrub growing along the bank to give him some screening.

He could hear Quintero's men coming down the arroyo now. He glanced at the sorrel's saddle scabbard and saw the butt of a carbine sticking out of it. He jerked it free and saw it was a '96 model Krag-Jorgensen. This was the carbine used by the cavalry just before the new Springfields. He hoped it was loaded. If it was, it had five .30-.40 cartridges in the magazine under the bolt, which wasn't a hell of a lot if you were trying to fight off a half-dozen Mexican guerrillas.

He reined up and turned and studied the mouth of the arroyo behind him. One of Quintero's men showed. Matt lifted the carbine, fired, and saw the man fly out of the saddle.

The others must have bunched up, sliding to a halt, but a pair of them got pushed out into the open. The sorrel stood steady as Matt aimed the carbine and shot again and missed. The horse was not gun-shy, he thought. He's got used to a lot of shooting.

He shot again, and the exposed pair pivoted and disappeared back into the arroyo. Matt turned up the riverbed again and put the sorrel into a run.

There was a sharp curve in the river ahead, and he raced into it. He was pleased at the stamina of the horse; he knew it had been ridden hard since the raid on Gunlock. The mount was not really big enough for a man of Matt's size, but it was wiry, tough and well-gaited. Unless Quintero and his men were likewise mounted, he suddenly had hope he'd get away and return to face Quintero at better odds. Meet Quintero alone and kill him.

He rounded a turn in the steep cutbank and then saw the

big herd of cattle coming fast toward him. It was fifty yards ahead and spread clear across the width of the river bottom, most likely hazed along by Mexican vaqueros riding far behind.

He hauled back on the bit and the sorrel slid to a stop so close to the forest of horns that he could almost touch them. The cattle in the lead tried to slow, but those behind pushed and kept coming.

His way was blocked. Panic took him. He glanced at the cutbank to his left and saw it was too steep to climb. He looked to his right and there was only open sand, an eighth of a mile across, studded here and there with boulders. Too much exposure to Quintero's fire.

And he could hear Quintero's shout as he spotted him. He heard the Quintero rifles crack, and a steer coming toward him flinched and staggered as a bullet struck it. But it stayed erect, held up by the thick press of those on either side.

He could see no way around and no way through.

He turned back to face Quintero, his anger making him reckless. A Quintero rifle cracked again, and he felt the red-hot sear rip through the deep flesh of his right thigh. His anger drained away—it was replaced by nausea and pain.

He turned the horse, kicked it with his left heel, and sent it angling across the front of the herd. Bullets spat the sand behind him.

Halfway across the bed the horse stumbled in the loose sand and threw him. He landed hard, crying out in pain but still clinging to the reins. He lay there, eyes closed, holding grimly to the tug of the sorrel.

When he could see again, he saw the herd splitting around him and saw he was in the protection of a large, round rock. A big steer, passing close, struck the staggering sorrel but missed with its horn. The horse went down. Matt caught the bridle close up, twisted the sorrel's neck, and pulled himself across its head to hold it down.

He heard the distant cries of Quintero's men as they lost sight of him in the rising dust and were cut off by the moving cattle. He lay there, suffocating and sick and hurt, fighting to hold the sorrel as it tried to rise. The cattle seemed to come forever. And then he heard the shouts of the trailing vaqueros as they rode past him, unseen in the roiling dust.

He let the sorrel get up, using it to pull himself to his feet. He cried out as his wounded thigh took his weight. The sorrel kept turning and making it impossible for him to mount, because he could not lift his right leg. He finally got hold of the big horn of the Mexican saddle and drew himself up high enough to get a foot in the stirrup. He gritted his teeth and dragged the bad leg up over the sorrel's rump and over the cantle.

The sorrel started to run again; he jerked, cursing, on the reins and the sorrel reared up, almost throwing him.

He got in the seat finally and turned upriver again. He looked once behind him and saw only the dust from the driven herd. He hoped Quintero and his men could not get around the barrier of horns.

He was getting weaker. Grimly, he held on to the horn of the saddle. He knew that if he fell he would never be able to mount again. He no longer tried to guide the sorrel. He let it have its head. It kept moving on up the riverbed in the direction from which the cattle had come, which seemed as good a way as any.

The shot came from the high east bank of the river. It was a lucky shot, lucky for Matt, because it missed and because it warned him that Quintero was still out there trying to kill him. Touching his left heel to the sorrel again, he turned west, away from the gunfire. The horse broke into a trot. Agony shot through his thigh; sweat broke out all over him.

He pulled the sorrel back into a walk, swearing. It was all Matt could handle without falling off. He waited for a bullet in the back as he walked the sorrel away from Quintero's riflemen on the steep bank.

No bullet came, and that surprised him. He twisted his neck and scanned the bank from which the rifle shot had come. He saw the reason then. There was another arroyo just beyond, and Quintero and his men were riding fast down it to the riverbed. It wouldn't take them more than a couple of minutes to overtake him.

He clenched his teeth and kicked the horse into a trot again. He hung on to the saddle horn with both hands, grunting in agony with each jarring step. A black haze filmed his vision. Behind him he could hear Quintero coming closer. He knew he couldn't get away. And he knew he couldn't get down from the horse now to fight.

He saw the far bank of the *río,* saw the screen of brush along its edge. If he could reach it in time. . . . The sorrel trotted on, laboring hard in the sandy bed. He went on and on and Matt could hear his own groans keep cadence with the sorrel's gait.

His sight was going. His hearing, too, because he could no longer hear Quintero's men coming after him.

He rode right into the crossing platoon of *federales* before he saw them, and he knew then why Quintero had stopped pursuing him.

"*Alto!*" The Mexican officer's tunic was trail-dirty and sweat-stained and his high collar was loosened. His stiff-visored cap was pulled low to shade his eyes from the sun's glare.

His mounted platoon halted at the command, and so did Matt.

Matt blinked, trying to focus on the *federales.* With the sorrel stopped, the pain eased in his thigh and his mind cleared slightly.

The *federale* officer said to nobody, "So what we have here is a gringo sergeant."

Matt had seen *federales* along the border, and he recognized the officer's insignia. *"Teniente,"* he said.

"Yes, I am lieutenant," the Carrancista said. "What are you doing in Mexico, gringo sergeant?"

Matt couldn't think of a quick answer that would explain anything.

The lieutenant said, "Answer when you are spoken to, gringo!"

"It is hard to explain," Matt said. He threw a quick look over his shoulder. There was no sign of Quintero and his men.

"You speak Spanish," the officer said. He studied the blood soaking through Matt's trouser leg. "I am Lieutenant Borquez. I demand to know what a gringo soldier is doing in Mexico."

Behind him and to his right, a man with the insignia of a sergeant said, *"Mi teniente,* the gringo is wounded."

Borquez said, "I recognize blood when I see it, *sargento.* Even gringo blood." Then to Matt he said, "Answer me!"

Matt said, "Last night . . . maybe the night before,"—he could not remember—"Villa's men raided a town in New Mexico."

"So?"

"We chased them back across the border and—"

"Into Mexico? You *maldito* gringo soldiers think you can come into our country?"

Matt felt his weakness growing. He said lamely, "We did not chase them far."

"Not far?" The Carrancista lieutenant pulled a map from his tunic. "It happens that we are on our way to the border. To Palomas, in fact. Right on the border. Do you know why? We are going there to see that none of your army violates our territory."

Matt felt his own rancor growing. "It appears you are too late, no?"

"You are forty miles into Mexico, gringo. Why are you wearing an American army uniform, forty miles inside Mexico?"

Matt shook his head.

The sergeant behind Borquez seemed to have some feeling for Matt, perhaps because he was of similar rank. He said, "The gringo could bleed to death, *teniente.*"

"That is no concern of mine," Borquez said. "Nor of yours."

Matt struggled to find the words, then said, "You are fighting against Villa, no? He is your enemy. Well, we were fighting Villistas, too."

The *federale* sergeant said, "Is that where you got your wound?"

Matt nodded.

The lieutenant said, "We Mexicans can fight our own battles. We do not need your help. We will not have you coming into Mexico as if you own us."

"There are six Villistas behind me," Matt said. "Chasing me."

The *federale* looked beyond Matt to the far bank of the river. "I see no one," he said.

"Six Villistas would be a good number, *mi teniente,*" the sergeant said. "We would have them outnumbered nicely."

"We are crossing the river here," Borquez said. "If we run into them, well and good. But I have my orders. To reach Palomas by tomorrow evening." He paused and frowned at Matt. "Anyway, I think this gringo is lying."

Matt shook his head again. He was getting dizzy and was afraid he was going to fall out of the saddle.

"What I think," the *teniente* continued, "is that this gringo sergeant is a deserter from his own army. I have only contempt for deserters."

"He has been in a fight, *mi teniente*," his sergeant said.

"He could have been shot by his own comrades. Even the gringos do that to their deserters."

"I do not hate gringos," his sergeant said. "Can we help this one from dying, *mi teniente?*"

"Well, *sargento mío, I* do not *like* gringos. I do not like deserters, either. I could help him by putting him out of his misery with a bullet."

"He says he has been fighting Villistas."

"On Mexican soil."

"We have some bandages, *mi teniente*. To stop the flow of blood, eh?"

"There is a possibility that he is telling the truth," the *teniente* said.

"*Con su permiso, teniente?* With your permission?"

"Get on with it, then. But stop the leak of blood only. Then he is on his own. We have no time to waste on a shot-up gringo."

CHAPTER 5

IT was a single-room adobe, and the narrow bed he was lying on took up most of it. There was a throbbing ache in his head and he dimly remembered the scalp wound, which was old now and hadn't pained him noticeably during the long, shock-filled hours after he'd found Molly.

There was other pain, too—around his ankles, where the bond tied by the charro had cut deep into his flesh. And there was great soreness in the flesh of his right thigh, and he remembered the liquid running down his leg and his wondering if it was blood from his wound or urine from his fear. Christ knows! he thought, he'd had reason for fear, what with six of them—or was it only five then?—only one jump behind him, and him with only a cartridge or two left in the Krag-Jorgensen.

A single window opening was covered by a splintered wood shutter, but enough daylight came into the room to make visible the dirt floor and a chair and a table against the wall opposite from where he lay. The room was so small he could almost have reached out and touched the table, if he hadn't felt so sore.

He tried to sit up and felt his head strike the adobe wall behind him as he fell back on the bunk.

When he awoke the next time it was dark and he could see nothing and he lay there, not moving, and wondered where he was.

There was sound from the closed door and he twisted his neck and saw the rectangle of lesser darkness as the door opened and the space filled with a slender figure, quickly blotted out as the door was shut again. There was the scratching from where the table was and then a match flared and lit a candle stuck to a dish and he could see the girl, and she was turning toward him.

She leaned over him, her breasts filling a low-cut loose blouse that was tucked into the slim waist of her skirt. Because the candle was behind her and her face was in shadow, he could not make out her features.

"*Cómo te sientes?*" she said softly. "How do you feel?"

"*Bien.*" he said, although he did not feel *bien* at all.

"That is good," she said, "Mateo."

"Mateo!" he said. "How is it you know my name?" He tried to raise himself up to get a better look.

"Lie back, Mateo, you gringo fool," she said. She bent closer so he could see her face, olive-tinged, and her dark eyes and her full mouth smiling faintly at him.

He began to remember. Four years back. Right after the fight at Tlahualilo, where they'd overrun Orozco's rear guard, forced a fight, and scattered the Redflaggers. Afterward Villa had ordered all the prisoners shot and had lined them up in bunches three-deep.

"That way we save ammunition," Villa had said. And he'd had his firing squad go down the line killing the Orozquistas three at a time with a single rifle bullet.

That was when Matt had seen enough. That was when he had left Villa.

He had left Juanita too. His *soldadera*, who had fought at his side for those many months.

"You remember now, Mateo?"

"I remember," he said.

Her lips stopped smiling and took on a pout. "Then say my name."

"Juanita," he said. He withdrew his hand from under the blanket that covered him and clasped her hand.

"That is better," she said.

He was silent, enjoying again the feel of her. Then he said, "What happened?"

"To you? You came riding an *alazán* horse the morning of two days ago. And fell from the saddle near the pool in the *río* where I was washing clothes. On my way home I found you and dragged you into the *matorral* where the bushes were thickest and wiped out all the markings. And just in time, too. It was lucky the *alazán*, the sorrel, ran off."

"How was it lucky?"

"Five riders came following you. I tell you, Mateo, I held my breath that you did not moan in pain there in the *matorral*."

He thought about this, and he was glad he hadn't, too.

"They asked if I had seen a gringo sergeant and I told them no."

"They believed you?"

"You are here, Mateo, no? I have learned to lie well these past few years. They paused only for a drink in the cantina here in Cobán. Perhaps they had to catch up with others."

"Cobán?" he said. "What is Cobán?"

"Just a little town."

"You live here?"

She shook her head. "I live far south, in Parral. No, Mateo, I am visiting my sister. She has been ill with child, but today she is better. Last night she gave birth. This room"—she gestured around her—"is separate from her house, but behind it."

"You were busy, then, last night," he said and lay back and closed his eyes, feeling the weakness come over him.

"Two sick ones," she said. "But both now getting better."

"That I should fall into your hands," he said.

"*Sí!*" she said. Then, so softly he wasn't sure she said it: "And that you should fall into my arms, Mateo—again."

But he was already sleeping.

He did not knowingly speak to her again through a succession of periods of daylight and darkness, when sometimes a candle burned by the bed and a shadow leaned over and pressed cool wet cloths to his face and body. Sometimes Molly seemed there and he spoke to her of his love and then cried out when he saw her die before his feverish eyes.

Then there came a day when he awoke and his mind was clear and Juanita was shaking him awake. He opened his mouth to speak and she pressed her palm hard against it.

"Mateo!" she whispered. "For the love of God do not cry out again. There are soldiers here in Cobán."

He reached her arm and pulled her hand away. He said in a low tone, "Villistas or *federales?*"

"Neither. Americans. *Norteamericanos.*"

"Americans?"

"They came into Cobán two hours ago. *Caballería.* Cavalry. I went to the cantina so I could hear what was happening. Already much is known."

"You went in the cantina?"

"Mateo! for the love of the Cristo, will you listen?" She gave him a fretful look, then her expression saddened. "Yes, I went in the cantina. Did you know I work in a cantina in Parral? And here, too, part of the time."

"I'm sorry," he said. "Go on."

"This is what happened—no, first I must tell you that you were delirious and talking wildly these past few days. There was an infection in the wound in your leg, I think. It is gone now—I hope."

"What about the soldiers?" he said.

"A week ago—on the same night you lost your woman—"

"You know?"

"—in the raid on Gunlock, there was a bigger raid on a town called Columbus. Many Americans were killed there, it is said, and your government took action *muy rápido*. Already your army has invaded us. A *brigada* of five thousand men, it is said, under the American general Pershing."

"Here in Cobán?"

"No. Here is only a provisional squadron under a major. And I heard talk in the cantina that there is a sergeant of the 12th Cavalry wanted for desertion." She looked at him with apprehension. "That is why I tore your sergeant's stripes from your shirt." She gestured at his uniform, which she had laundered and hung over the back of the chair.

Matt looked, and he could see the dark outlines on the faded sleeves where his chevrons had been. "Goddamit, Juanita, that's not going to fool anybody!"

"Do not swear at me, Mateo!"

"Sorry," he said. "You saved my life and I'm grateful. But what you did to my sleeves, that isn't enough. I've got to get some civilian clothes."

"But you have no money left, Mateo. I had to spend what I found in your pockets."

"All right. Go on about the soldiers."

"They are going to set up camp near the south end of Cobán by the river." She hesitated, then said, "They are of the 12th Regiment—your own. Can you not go back to them? Is one single week considered desertion?"

He shrugged. "There is a reason I will not go back."

"You seek the *capitán*, Quintero. Because of your woman."

He nodded. He must have blabbed the whole story in his delirium, he thought. "It was Quintero and his men who shot me. Who questioned you at the river the day you saved my life. You did not know him from when you were with Villa?"

She shook her head. "I did not know Quintero. But I will help you find him so that you may have your revenge."

"Why?"

"Because you want it," she said simply.

There was the sound of mounted men moving past. She went to the door and opened it a crack. "They are riding by," she said.

He sat up, twisted around, got his bare feet on the floor, and forced himself to stand. He swayed there, struck by dizziness, until she hurried to him, then he leaned on her and she led him to the door. He looked out and recognized the men of the squadron, with Major Holcomb in the lead.

They were combat-ready, he thought. Their uniforms and equipment were 1912 issue: olive drab shirts with flap pockets and breeches that flared at the hips. Canvas leggings or leather boots. Peaked olive drab campaign hats with wide brims and chin straps. Ammunition belts and .45 automatic pistols in holsters low on the right leg. Ninety rounds of ammunition in pockets on the belts.

They sat in McClellan saddles and their saddlebags carried two days' ration of hard bread, bacon, coffee, sugar and mess kit.

Across their pommels each carried a grain bag with two days' forage of corn for his horse. Blanket and shelter half rolled at the cantle. Springfield rifles carried in boots. And bayonets strapped behind left shoulders.

They passed quickly on the way to the bivouac area. He began to feel weak, went to the chair, and sat down, rumpling the uniform she had placed there.

Juanita moved to his side and tugged the uniform free and folded it again, smoothing out the creases with her hand. "I will get you other clothes, Mateo," she said.

"How?" he said. Then he just nodded weakly and walked unsteadily to the bed.

When he next awoke there were the clothes of an American cowboy laid nearby, and she was watching him.

"How did you afford these?" he said. "You had no money. What did you trade for them?"

"I traded nothing for them, Mateo. Not my body, if that is what you think. Now that you are back with me I will be a good girl again."

"Then how did you get them?" There was exasperation in his voice.

"I did not trade, I tell you! I am a good girl again—I stole them."

He shook his head slowly. "Ay! Juanita!" Then he said, "But they are of the American style—why?"

She looked at him pityingly. "Do you think I would steal from a Mexican?" she said.

"Put on the clothes, Mateo," she said.

He began slowly pulling them on. They were worn but freshly washed, which surprised him. She had judged his size or maybe just been lucky, because they fit well — Levi's, gray wool shirt and a sheepskin jacket. When he was fully dressed, still wearing his own boots and hat, he posed in front of her.

"*Magnífico!*" she said. "You will pass now for some gringo vaquero who works for a rich *hacendado.*"

"Just like the poor bastard they belonged to," he said. "Tell me, where did you steal them?"

"Beyond the cantina there is a barber who also rents tubs of hot water for taking baths. That is what the American cowboy was doing. And he paid to have his clothes washed by the wife of the *barbero.* And she had them hanging outside to dry and—"

"Enough!" he said. "But I cannot wear them in this town."

"We must leave Cobán as soon as it is dark," she said. "We will go to Parral, for that is where we will find word of Villa's men. Perhaps of Quintero. Now that the Americans have come hunting them, they will hide in the south. And

we will be away from this crazy major of yours who charges
you with desertion."

"*De acuerdo,*" he said. "Agreed."

She looked at him, weighing something in her mind. "I
will be your *soldadera* again, Mateo?"

"*Mi soldadera,*" he said. "My soldier girl."

"That was a time, eh, Mateo?"

"It was a time," he said. "And after I left? After I no
longer fought for Villa?"

"I went with another. What did you expect?"

"Of course, it was the custom," he said. But he felt a
touch of jealousy. He thought back to how it was, how the
women of the peasant soldiers accompanied their men.
Pots and pans and bedding strapped on their backs, children sometimes clinging to their skirts.

Sometimes they fought alongside the men, earning the
title of *soldadera.* If a *soldadera* lost her man in battle, she
would spend a night or two in grief, then take another.

"I thought many times about how it was with us, Mateo.
At Juárez, where we met, and after." She paused. "The
year after you left there was much killing." She paused
again. "I lost three men in that year. One after another. I
began to feel like the whore of death. That's when *I* quit
Villa."

He did not know what to say.

"Now that I have you back, Mateo, it will be different.
When the wound in your thigh is fully healed, I will show
you."

Still he was silent.

Just south of Cobán the troopers of the 12th were making
camp. As the sun dropped, the air grew cold. They lit their
fires and went about cooking their rations.

Major Holcomb was in his tent poring over a map, studying the approach to Casas Grandes, sixty miles south,
where he was to rendezvous with the main body of the

expedition that had entered Mexico from Culberson's Ranch, New Mexico. Holcomb's understanding was that the first operational base would be set up in Casas Grandes while Pershing made a field decision as to how to best deploy his brigade to capture Villa.

Major Holcomb was eager to get to Casas Grandes and begin the hunt. The trail of Villa's guerrillas was now a week old, and although Holcomb had left Gunlock behind him, he'd had word before he left that there would be a board of inquiry looking into his possible negligence in defending the town.

A blot on his record no matter how it turned out, he thought. He scowled to himself, then shrugged impatiently. One thing could erase that blot in a hurry—getting Villa. Erase the blot hell!—there'd damn sure be a promotion for him. And not just a silver oak leaf, either, but a jump to the silver eagles of a full-bird colonel—he'd bet on it. Holcomb had wanted those eagles so long he could feel them on his shoulders.

His dog-robber, Private Oursler, entered the tent to serve his meal. That done, he stood back waiting uncomfortably, as if he had something to say but didn't know if he should.

Holcomb sensed this and said, "What is it, Oursler?"

"Begging your pardon, sir, but I just heard something you might want to know."

"Well, out with it, man!"

"Well, sir, I ain't one to snitch on one of our own, sir," the orderly said, "but one of the troopers come in staggering drunk a few minutes ago from the town. Drunker'n a lord he is, sir. That's what this Mexican tequila can do to you, they say, sir—"

"Goddamit!" Holcomb said. "Get on with it!"

"—Yes, sir. Well, I reckon he'll get company punishment aplenty for dropping off in the cantina like that, eh, sir? Being AWOL, ain't it, sir?"

"Oursler!"

"Oh, yes, sir. Well, it seems he picked up some information I thought you might be wanting to hear, sir."

Holcomb gave up and waited.

"It seems there's knowledge around town, sir, among the Mexicans, that a wounded American sergeant has been holed up in Cobán for a week more or less. There's a Mexican girl been hiding him and nursing him and—"

"Sergeant Dunn!" Holcomb rasped.

"—Quite likely it is, sir."

"Who is the drunk that got this information?"

Oursler made only a token hesitation. "Private Norberg, sir." Oursler had to fight to keep the satisfaction out of his voice. Private Oursler and Private Norberg were not best friends: a drunken Norberg had nearly broken Oursler's ribs with a single smash of his big fist back in Gunlock. Private Norberg had called Oursler a dog-robbing kiss-ass. Oursler resented the accusation intensely, because it had made him wonder if it might be true.

"Have Private Norberg brought in to me," Holcomb said. "Now!"

"I need a horse," Matt said. "We both need horses."

"We have horses," Juanita said. "My brother-in-law caught your sorrel the day after he ran away. And he has given me another."

"Was there a carbine in the saddle scabbard?"

"The carbine, yes. And I found extra cartridges in a saddlebag."

"I lost my handgun back there when Quintero tried to have me trampled."

She went to a box in a corner of the room. She brought back an army Colt .45 revolver in a Mexican holster and belt. "Remember? You gave me this yourself, right after Juárez. You took it off a dead Porfirista."

He took the gun and belt from her and hefted it. He held it around his waist, but the belt was several inches too short. He tried to shove the revolver into his .45 automatic flap holster, but it wouldn't fit.

"Well," Juanita said, "you have the carbine. I will use the *pistola*."

"You can get in trouble doing that," he said.

"I am a *soldadera*," she said. "Never forget that."

In the darkness, Juanita's brother-in-law brought the horses, and Matt met him for the first time.

"*Buena suerte, sargento*," the brother-in-law said. "Good luck. I call myself Pilo and I ask your pardon that I have not sooner made myself known to you. But there are reasons. It is not prudent in these times for a man of Chihuahua to knowingly harbor a *norteamericano*. There are the Villistas and the Carrancistas and even your own countrymen who could make trouble for us. But now I wish luck to you and this favorite sister-in-law of mine."

"*Adios, cuñado*," Juanita said. "And take care of my little sister, you hear?"

Pilo handed her a small leather pouch. "Coins," he said. "Not much, but enough for food on the way."

"*Gracias por todos*," Matt said. "Thanks for everything."

"*Vámonos!*" Juanita said. "I will be more content when we have left your *caballería* behind." She swung up easily into the saddle, and even in the shadows Matt could see the tightness of the charro pants she had dressed herself in. She had a charro jacket, too, and over her shoulder a serape of the Saltillo style.

She turned east, and within a few minutes they came to the river. At this time of the year, before the heavy rains of summer struck the peaks of the Sierra Madre, the river was mostly dry except for shallow streams and pools in the lowest parts of its bed. There was no moon, but the shine from the stars lit the dry sand of the bottom. Matt felt his nervousness grow. If anybody's looking we're like targets in a shooting gallery, he thought. How wide is this goddam riverbed, anyway?

Major Holcomb had seen his first action in '98 at San Juan Hill as a shavetail just out of West Point. He had done two tours in the Philippines under Pershing and had survived a *bolo* knife slash across the abdomen while bayoneting a crazed Moro at Jolo. He wasn't an armchair soldier: he loved action when he was in it and craved it when he was not.

If that damn upcoming board of inquiry at Gunlock — well, whatever their decision was, they would never find he lacked in aggressive courage. Lacked prudence, perhaps. Negligent sometimes, maybe. But, goddamit, it was lack of action that could wear away at a man's discretion until he sometimes got careless, they ought to know that.

So when he had finished interrogating Private Norberg, who had fallen on his face twice while trying to stand at attention, Holcomb decided he would personally take charge of a detail to haul in Sergeant Dunn.

He remanded Norberg to the custody of the waiting first sergeant of C Troop. "What punishment shall I give him, sir?" the first sergeant said. "Binding and gagging with a bar of issue soap in his mouth?"

"Nothing that drastic, Sergeant," the major said. "If he hadn't got drunk we wouldn't know about Dunn." He paused. "Get me a detail of six men. I'm going to arrest that deserter now."

"Yes, sir."

"And send that cowboy, Lacy, to me — that American I hired this afternoon as a civilian scout."

Lacy was the first to appear. "Major," he said.

The major studied him thoughtfully. Lacy looked like a thousand other cowboys he'd seen along the border. Lean and tanned and tough and somewhere in his thirties. But there were two things about him that set him apart from most.

One, Lacy had worked cattle for years down here in Mexico, both for wealthy American ranchers and for Mexican *hacendados*. Or so he had said when he'd asked for the job as guide and scout.

Two, despite his weathered gringo looks, he was wearing a Mexican vaquero's clothes and they were spanking new.

Holcomb frowned. "Why the costume, Lacy? You look got-up for a masquerade ball."

Lacy scowled. "Nothing like that, Major. It's just that after I talked to you about this scouting job I went to get a bath and some sonofabitch stole my clothes."

Holcomb's frown deepened, but he said, "There's a deserter from my command hiding in that town, Lacy—"

"I heard about that, Major."

"I want you to go in there and find out where he's hid."

"I got a few friends around Cobán, Major. That shouldn't be too hard to do."

"And report back here to me as soon as you know."

Lacy gave a lax salute and went out.

He was back at the camp in half an hour.

Holcomb was waiting. So was the arrest detail—six privates and Lieutenant Darwin of D Troop, who had pleaded to go along.

"You got to hurry, Major," Lacy said. "They just pulled out—Sergeant Dunn and the Mexican girl together. And I caught sight of them and trailed them to where they started across the river. The girl's from Parral, so my guess is they'll be heading south. There's a pretty good trail runs along the other side there, nothing like the road on this side but pretty good."

"We'll cross right here, then," Holcomb said, "and intercept them."

CHAPTER 6

ONCE across the sandy, starlit expanse that had worried Matt, Juanita turned onto the trail, which threaded along a screening of *álamos*. To their left Matt could see the dark blur of what appeared to be thick chaparral.

After a few minutes she stopped and he pulled up beside her.

"One thing I must know," she said. "If we should have to face your army *compañeros*, would you fight them?"

He had been troubled by the same thought. Now it was out there confronting him, and he had to decide. "Will we run into them?"

"I hope not. But if we should?"

"I could not kill a comrade," he said. "Not even to escape."

"I was afraid of that," she said. "Ay, Mateo! You make things doubly hard for us."

"That is the way it has to be."

"All right, then," she said, and they began to ride again.

She rode slowly for a ways, only now he could see her head turned often toward the chaparral to the east. She seemed to be looking for something.

Suddenly she stopped and turned into the heavy growth. He followed, and almost at once he felt the clutch of sharp brambles and the sting of a cactus spike on his leg. He began to swear.

She stopped again and he rode into her horse in the darkness and swore again.

"*Cállate!* Shut up!" she said. "Sound carries far along the *río*. Do you think your major is deaf?"

"This goddam brush—"

"Of course. This is *malpais. Matorral.* Full of cactus. Prickly pear and jumping *cholla* and up ahead the *garambullo* cactus grows higher than a horse's head. And all mixed in with mesquite."

"Then how—?"

"I grew up in Cobán," she said. "As a child I learned a way through this *malpais.* A narrow trail, not much used, once only the wandering path of some strayed cattle perhaps. It is maybe twelve kilometers long."

"And on the other end?"

"There is another road south toward Casas Grandes."

"But why did you turn in here?"

"You said you would not fight against your comrades."

He had no answer for that.

"Well?" she said.

"Go ahead," Matt said.

Without another word she started to inch forward, moving blindly, it seemed to him.

But after a mile or so he could tell she was following some sort of path, although he could not understand how she could see it in the shoulder-high blackness.

A partial moon appeared in the east to guide them, but its light did not penetrate down to the trail. Branches of tall mesquite stabbed at the eyes of the horses, and her mount balked and refused to go on.

She slipped down from the saddle. "We will have to walk and lead the horses," she said.

But then she did not move.

"What's wrong?"

"Listen!"

He listened, but at first all he could hear was the heavy breathing of the sorrel.

Then, faintly, he could hear them coming from back by the river.

When she spoke again there was puzzlement in her voice. "Whoever follows knows the trail. It would have to be somebody from Cobán."

"Let's go," he said.

She started off again leading her mount and he came behind leading the sorrel. Behind them it was no longer hard to hear the troopers. Their curses carried even through the muffling growth of the *matorral*. It seemed to Matt that the sound was coming closer. He called ahead to her, *"Andale, ándale!"*

But she did not change her pace.

They pushed their torturous way for an hour without stopping. His face was scratched and stung from flailing branches and there were cactus punctures and probably cactus spines in a dozen places on his body. He was weakening from the effects of his wounds, and the one in his leg had become a throbbing source of agony. He clamped his jaws to keep from crying out at every step.

"This place is a goddam pincushion," he said once.

If Juanita heard him, she ignored him.

All at once he was aware of some change that bothered him. "Juanita!"

She stopped and tried to peer back around her horse, which was completely blocking the trail.

"I no longer hear the soldiers," he said.

They both stood listening. There was no noise behind them now.

"Maybe they turned back," he said.

"Perhaps," she said. "The way would be rough for a gringo soldier."

"Tell me about it," he said. Then: "How much farther for us?"

"We are maybe halfway."

He groaned. "Well, we lost them anyway. Keep going. I can't get out of this needlestack soon enough."

She began moving again, and now, it seemed to him, she was moving faster.

He could no longer keep up. He was getting faint from weakness. For a man just out of bed and not yet fully recuperated, it was too much.

He wanted to call out to her to stop, but her own toughness shamed him into silence. He was counting each step now, each time he put his weight down on his aching leg. He was slowing and the sorrel slowed with him and she pulled ahead, not noticing, and left him behind.

He cursed and threw the reins up over the sorrel's neck and hauled himself into the saddle, ignoring the brambles that caught at his jacket. He kicked at the sorrel, forcing it forward although he could not see ahead.

He could not see Juanita, either, and after five minutes he reined up and he knew he had left the trail, that he was lost in the maze of the *matorral*. The sorrel stood quiet, waiting. He felt panic. He listened hard and thought he could hear the girl far ahead of him and to the south. He called out then but got no answer.

He got the horse moving again in the direction from which he believed he'd heard the sound. But now the way was even harder, since he had no trail at all to follow. The sorrel, though, at his urging kept forging away. He felt a sudden affection for it. It was truly a horse far better than most.

The sorrel plodded on, picking its way now through the high *garambullo* cactus, flinching sometimes as the spines drove in, following along a course of least resistance. That this could be dangerous, could get him so hopelessly lost that he might die in the *malpais*, he was aware. But he had no choice.

Now he began to hope that Juanita did not notice he was not following. Because if she did, she might turn back looking for him and lose herself.

What a hell of a mess, he thought. All on account of that goddam major.

Juanita had continued on her way for half an hour before she paused to rest and noticed that Matt was not behind her. She waited, expecting him to catch up, and when he didn't she became worried. The *malpais* had taken the lives of many people of Cobán over the years, and it was nothing to be taken lightly.

Still, she judged that she was only a few hundred yards away from breaking out onto the other road to Casas Grandes. While she was debating what to do she thought she heard Matt moving far back of her, but north of the trail. She decided to continue to the road and ride north on it, hoping to make voice contact with him from there. She was afraid to call to him now, not being sure whether the soldiers had really given up the chase.

She started on again.

Her judgment was correct, and within a few minutes she broke out of the *matorral* and there in front of her was the road, a silver ribbon of dust in the moonlight. The way was clear.

She stepped out into the open.

And a voice with an American cowboy's twang said, "*Arriba las manos, muchacha!* Up with the hands!" Then: "We got the girl, Major!"

Juanita did not hesitate. She jerked the revolver from her holster and fired two fast shots into the air.

A trooper came from behind and clubbed down on her gun hand with the barrel of his carbine, knocking the weapon from her grasp.

Matt was still thrashing around blindly in the *matorral* when he heard the shots. They came from close by and a little south of him. Juanita! He kicked at the sorrel and it blundered head-on into a clump of the cursed *garambullo* and shied backward, squealing its pain.

It was several minutes before he could force it forward. By then he had a grip on himself and let it pick its own way again, guiding it in the general direction from which the shots had sounded.

Was it only a signal to guide him? he wondered. Or had that goddam major outsmarted them after all?

Unexpectedly he burst out of the brush and into the open, and he saw the roadway. Immediately he wheeled the horse and tried to ride it back into the cover of the *matorral*. It refused to move no matter how hard he drove his heels into its flanks.

Well, I don't blame you, he thought, and gave up the losing effort. He turned and peered down the road. He thought he could see shadows moving about in the gloom, by the road's borders.

He knew then that Juanita was in trouble. The absolute quiet after the firing of the shots told him that. His immediate problem was how to approach the area where he believed her to be. He could not ride openly down the road in the moonlight. And he couldn't force the sorrel back into the brush and so try to work nearer.

He had to leave the horse.

He dismounted and tugged it, resisting, close enough to the fringe of the *matorral* to tie it to a branch of mesquite. The sorrel had developed such a dislike for the thorny growth that it kept backing off, trying to pull loose, its rump well out into the road.

"Goddamit, horse!" he said. "Hang still!"

As if it understood, the sorrel all at once relaxed and moved in until the tied reins were slack.

"That's better," Matt said. His thigh was throbbing again and he kneaded it with his fingers, but that made it hurt worse. Well, he couldn't worry about that. He shoved the feeling of pain from his mind and slithered back into the maze of cactus. And was immediately stuck again.

If the way through the *malpais* by trail and been torturous walking, it was nothing compared with what he now endured. He hadn't gone ten yards before he knew it was impossible.

He slipped again onto the road, walked back, and untied the horse. The moon had swung toward the west enough that there was a narrow border of dark along the road's edge, though scarcely wide enough to screen a mounted man.

He stayed in the dark border as best he could, leading the horse again. The sorrel kept swinging out into the road, and he knew it would not take much for it to be seen by anybody with eyesight better than that of a myopic *javelina* pig.

The agony of his leg came back, and finally he said the hell with it and pulled himself into the saddle and rode the sorrel again. He pulled the Krag-Jorgensen carbine from its scabbard and held it cocked and ready.

He could no longer see any moving shadows and he had lost track of the spot where he thought he'd seen them before. Things weren't getting any better, he thought.

And at that moment they got worse.

He heard Juanita scream not more than a hundred feet ahead. A Springfield cracked and the shot went by his right ear so close he felt the wind from it. Instinctively he wheeled the sorrel to the left and crossed the road, the horse leaping as it took the spurs. He plunged into the brush, braced for the shock of cactus spines, and was surprised when he felt none.

He should have thought of that before. Nobody would have carved a road through the *matorral*. It obviously ran along the edge. And the brush on this side was only mesquite and greasewood.

Juanita, held from behind by a youthful trooper pressing a .45 into her ribs and a calloused palm over her mouth, had seen Matt riding down the road to where they were waiting for him.

She wanted to cry out and she couldn't. She tried to squirm loose and felt the gun muzzle ram into her flesh so hard she sickened.

But she knew something of young men, and she did not believe the trooper would pull the trigger. Not the way he was holding her body tight against his, as if he were enjoying the feel of it. She gambled on this and raised her leg as far as she could, kicked back, and roweled her sharp Mexican spur through his canvas legging. Once again she was the battle-tested *soldadera*.

The young trooper grunted in pain and loosened his grip over her mouth. She twisted her head and snapped her teeth on his finger. He raised his gun and clubbed it at her head, but he was so close the impact only sent her partway to her knees. As his hand came free from her bite she gave her warning scream, grabbed up her own gun from where it lay in the dust, and dove into the *matorral*. She heard some nervous trooper fire a rifle at Matt.

Behind her the soldiers were swearing in their confusion and she could hear the one who was the major barking orders in *inglés*. She turned to her left as the thorns tore at her, crawled a few yards, then turned again out onto the road. She glanced back, saw the figures of the soldiers mill ing about, and took a chance and ran across to the less hostile brush of the other side.

And ran into Matt on the sorrel, breaking his way through the mesquite.

He recognized her, or thought he did, and said, "Juanita? Get up here behind me!"

"There are nine of them, Mateo! Eight soldiers and one gringo cowboy."

"They got your horse?"

"*Sí.*"

"We got to get it. We'll never get away riding two on one."

"How?"

The major stepped over to the youthful private, who was hopping around with his left hand tucked under his right armpit. "Stop caterwauling! I can't hear where the hell either one of them is now."

Lieutenant Darwin said, "I think he crossed the road, sir."

"The girl went back into the cactus," Lacy said. "I saw her break for it."

"Why didn't you stop her?"

"How? I'm being paid to guide you, Major, not shoot Mexican girls."

"Some guide," the major said.

"I showed you a way around the *malpais*, didn't I? And had you waiting for the girl when she came out."

"All right," Holcomb said. "The hell with it. I'm not going to chase all over this goddam country all the goddam night. Guide us back to Cobán."

They mounted and Darwin said, "What about the girl's horse, sir?"

"Lead it, Lieutenant. Lead it, goddamit!"

"Yes, sir," the lieutenant said. He rode close to Juanita's mount and caught up the trailing reins.

They strung along single file, heading down the road.

Lacy dropped back beside Darwin, who was bringing up the rear. "This Sergeant Dunn," he said, "he sure seems to be a burr under the major's rear."

"That's true, Lacy."

"What I gather—I mean, I heard about how the sergeant lost his wife at Gunlock—well, I ain't a army man, but I sure can't fault him for taking after that Mexican on his own."

"The army has its regulations," Darwin said. "That makes a difference."

"I reckon so. Still—how do you feel about it, Lieutenant?"

Darwin rode on a little before he answered. He kept his voice low, making sure the major, up front, couldn't hear him. "He's one of my own men, Lacy. He fought beside me at Gunlock, and they don't come any better. He has my sympathy. If ever I can testify in his behalf, I will do what I can for him."

"If he is ever caught."

Darwin rode in silence again, then he sighed. "The major will catch him," he said finally. "You can count on it."

Matt, with Juanita mounted behind him on the sorrel, peered through the screening of mesquite and saw Holcomb's men riding past. He could not make out their individual identities, but he could tell that a led horse was bringing up the rear and knew that it had to be Juanita's.

He had shoved the Krag into its scabbard, and now he reached back and jerked her six-gun from its holster. He shoved it into his waistband and slipped down off the mount. "Get in the saddle," he whispered and handed her the reins.

She climbed over the cantle and let her feet hang above the long stirrups.

He slipped into the roadway and took the gun in his hand. Five fast steps and he was beside the man leading Juanita's horse. He stuck the six-gun's barrel into the man's side.

"All right," he said in a low voice. "Let go the reins and don't get foolish, trooper."

"Christ! Dunn! It's me, Darwin!"

For a second Matt was dumb. Then he said, "Sorry, Lieutenant. But I got to have the horse."

Darwin had halted, and now he handed the reins to Matt. The column was moving away from them, nobody looking back. "You may be making another mistake, Matt."

"It's got to be, Lieutenant."

"I suppose."

Matt swung up on the horse, still keeping Juanita's gun pointed at the officer. "Give me one minute to get off the road—"

"Sure," Darwin said.

Just then Lacy, who had started up the column, turned his head and saw Darwin stopped back there; he turned his horse and raced back.

Matt saw him coming, aimed the gun at him, then hesitated. He could not shoot a comrade, no matter what.

Lacy, too late, saw him mounted there in the shadows and saw the glint of the barrel of the gun. In desperation he drove his horse into Matt's.

The impact knocked them both half out of their saddles. Matt's arm swung wide as he strove for balance and his finger went tight on the trigger. The gun fired and he heard Lieutenant Darwin cry out and slump over his horse's neck.

Oh, God! he thought, I've shot the lieutenant!

And then Lacy triggered a shot of his own and the horse squealed as the slug gashed across its neck, and Matt wheeled it around and plunged again into the brush. He glimpsed Juanita in passing and then they were both racing through the mesquite with the man who had shot at him right behind.

The man was shooting at them, but Matt did not want to shoot back. He counted the shots and judged when the man's gun was empty. Then he turned and fired his own, firing wide of the target, and the man reined up, cursing.

"This way, Mateo!" Juanita called to him, and he turned and ran the horse after the sorrel.

Back in the column one of the troopers took a first aid packet from his belt and bandaged a flesh wound in Lieutenant Darwin's forearm.

Major Holcomb, watching, said, "There's another charge now against that bastard Dunn. Added to desertion is assault and attempted murder of a commissioned officer. He'll do a long stretch at Leavenworth for that."

CHAPTER 7

THEY reached the towns of Colonia Dublán and Casas Grandes. And the army of the punitive expedition was only a dozen miles behind them all the way.

Then to Galeana, where they heard in the plaza, while resting under the wilted, dusty trees, that the Americans had stopped at the Casas to set up headquarters. Now they knew they could take their time for the rest of the way.

Matt was ready for it. There had been that first night in the *malpais* and then three days more of hard riding to reach Galeana, and the wound in his thigh hurt constantly. It wore his nerves thin and made his temper with Juanita short.

He said, "We need grain for the horses. Find the livery stable." He did not want to talk to the natives. He did not like the sidelong glances they gave him from under their sombreros.

Juanita spoke a few words to one of them, then said, "Come, Mateo. The stable is down the street that goes behind the hotel."

At the stables an old Mexican came out, carrying a hay-fork.

Matt said, "Some corn for the horses, eh, *viejo?* And water, of course. But not too much, too fast. They have been hard ridden."

The old man had gray eyes, a thing that Matt thought was

always disconcerting when you first saw them down here. The old man's eyes studied Matt quickly, noting the way he favored his right leg. He said, "I can see they have been hard ridden. Shall I take their saddles off?"

"Why do you ask?"

The old man shrugged. He leaned his hayfork against a wall and took the horses by their reins.

"You think I might want to ride them hard again in a hurry, is that it?" Matt said.

"That depends, of course, on the urgency."

"We heard in the plaza that the Americans who entered Mexico have stopped at Casas Grandes," Matt said. "What do you know about this, *viejo?*"

"I have heard the same. The word reached Onate by telegraph. A rider from there brought us the news."

"In that case, unsaddle the horses."

"*Sí, señor.* They need that." The old man made another appraisal of Matt. "Would you believe it, señor, that at first I thought you were a gringo?" His words were slyly facetious.

"We all make mistakes, old one," Matt said, echoing his tone.

"That is the truth. But I will care well for the horses." He hesitated. "But they should have rest. If it is possible."

"It is possible," Matt said.

"If you, yourselves, would rest also, señor, I would recommend our hotel, which faces on the plaza."

Matt said, "We will consider it, *viejo. Gracias.*"

"*Por nada,*" the old man said. "It is nothing."

They turned back toward the plaza.

Juanita said, "The *viejo* has good advice, Mateo."

"In what way?"

"You should rest a night in the hotel. For the sake of your wound."

"Can we afford it?"

She nodded. "My brother-in-law was more generous than he implied. We can spare enough for one night. There will still be enough for food on the way to Parral."

"It is your money."

"Then I choose to stay at the hotel," she said. "With you, Mateo."

The room was dingy, like most rooms in the small-town hotels of Chihuahua. But there was a bed, and he lay back on it gratefully, groaning as he lifted his sore, stiff leg.

"Take off your pants," Juanita said.

"What?"

"I cannot tend your wound through your Levi's."

She poured water from a pitcher onto a cloth and bathed the wound. "Well, it is healing. Not as rapidly as it might. But we can travel slower now, and that will help."

Later she brought them up a meal from a restaurant.

As they ate, dusk came over the town. Matt got up and limped to the single window and looked into the plaza. People still loitered there, seeming to enjoy the quiet peace. The people of Chihuahua had learned during the past six years to do that every chance they got, he thought to himself. They were doing it now before the Americans came.

Later, in the dark, Juanita lay beside him and ran her fingers over his lean, tough body. He could feel her breath hot on his jaw. He knew she wanted him to make love to her. He knew that, and he tried, but his hurt wouldn't let him. The hurt of the wound in his leg. That and the pain of losing Molly.

In the morning, when they went to the stable to get the horses, he told Juanita to give the old man a tip. Then he said, "I would ask of you another question, old one. Have you seen five or six riders come through Galeana in this past week? The leader would be gaunt, with wide shoulders, and tall for a Mexican. He would be wearing a gun well."

"It makes now a full week, señor," the old man said. "But only five came through, not six. One, though, wore a mourner's armband. I heard this one talk about the recent shooting death of his cousin Flaco. By a gringo army sergeant."

"Those, possibly, could be the ones. And they were riding to . . . ?"

"South," the old man said. "I tell you this only because they refused to pay me for my services. And the gaunt one threatened to shoot me when I protested."

Matt watched the *viejo*'s face and said, "That one calls himself Captain Quintero. He rides with Villa."

"Quintero!" The old man's face showed nothing, but he crossed himself unconsciously.

"You know the name?"

"*Qué va!* Who does not?" the old man said. "Christ and the saints! And I argued with him!" He met Matt's eyes and his own took on a pleading look. He said, "Señor, please forget that I told you he passed through this town. That is, if he should ask you."

"We are not friends."

"Then may God be on your side if you meet him," the old man said.

El Valle. Las Cruces, Namiquipa, San Geronimo. Bachíniva, Agua Caliente and Cienégita. All Mexican towns, all with the same look.

There was a night somewhere south of Cienégita when they lay on their blankets under the stars, the air unusually warm for early spring in that high country.

"Mateo?"

"*Sí, chica.*"

"You don't know how much I missed you when you left. There was never another like you for me."

"Never another gringo, you mean," he said. He was sorry as soon as he said it.

He heard the intake of breath and then she was silent.

"I'm sorry," he said. "And I am sorry I cannot make love to you. Not now."

"Tell me about your woman," she said. "Perhaps it will help if you talk about her."

"No. Nothing will help."

"Even revenge?"

"I must have revenge. A chance for it, at least. Maybe revenge will help."

"You loved her much?"

"I loved her much. I had her only a month in all. Maybe that makes it hurt even worse."

"I'm sorry, Mateo."

He got up from his blanket and began to pace back and forth.

She said, watching, "Why will you risk your life against Quintero if it will not help?"

"I said it might help. But even if it does not, it is something I must do."

"Did you miss me, Mateo?"

"Many times. Many times I thought of you."

"But you never came back to find me."

"I never came back."

"Why?" She threw off the blanket that was covering her. "Stop pacing," she said, "and look at me, Mateo."

He stopped and looked at her lying there, naked and beautiful in the moonlight.

"It is no use, *chica*," he said. "I am sorry."

"But do you not need a woman yet, Mateo?"

He shook his head.

"You are still in love with your *gringa*," she said.

"It was different with her."

She covered herself again with her blanket. "Perhaps it is wrong for me to say, because I am only a cantina girl now. But I am jealous of her."

"Shut up!" he said. "I don't want to hear that. It was different with her!"

"All right, Mateo. Come back and sleep. I will not bother you anymore. Not tonight."

Three days later they reached Parral.

An antique mining town a mile high, surrounded by mountain deposits of silver, gold, lead and copper that had been worked by Indians and Mexicans for three hundred years. A quiet town until one or another faction of the Revolution took it, then let it go.

Juanita said, "We will stop first at the cantina where I worked."

Matt scowled. He did not like the idea. In Mexico, most of the girls who worked in the cantinas were *putas*.

She saw his scowl and said, "A girl has to eat."

"I have not asked before," he said, "but why have you not taken a husband?"

"After being *soldadera* to four different men?"

He looked at her, riding straight and proud in the saddle, her chiseled profile turned to him, the rich olive of her lean cheek, the firm fullness of her breasts undisguised by her charro jacket. "That cannot be the whole reason," he said. "That would not absolutely prevent it."

"I will, perhaps, tell you the reason, but at a later time," she said. She kept her eyes straight ahead.

She led him to a side street and reined up in front of the Cantina Chihuaheño. "Here is where I work," she said. "At least, I did until I went to visit my sister." She tied her horse to the rack in front of the place and he did likewise.

The cantina was empty of customers at this hour. A short, mustached ox of a man stood near the bar. There was some belly to him under his apron, but it was solid and had strength to it, Matt thought. A man *de panza*.

"*Qué pasó*, Juanita?"

"Rafael," Juanita said, "this is Mateo."

The *cantinero* extended his hand. "I call myself Gómez," he said. His eyes searched Matt's face closely. "What is your pleasure, señor?"

"At this hour I would choose coffee," Matt said.

The *cantinero* squinted in thought. "You have good Spanish, señor, but I cannot place the accent. However, the *café* can be had."

He left and presently returned to serve the coffee.

"Please, Rafael," Juanita said, "Mateo here desires to speak with you. Can you sit?"

Gómez sat.

"I will tell you, Rafael," she said. "Mateo was with Villa at the first Juárez and after. I was his *soldadera* in those days."

"*Es verdad*, señor? Is this the truth? Then I salute you. I place the accent now. *Norteamericano*, no?"

"As if you had doubt," Matt said.

"With Villa, eh? Then it was with the Gringo Legion?"

"The same."

"And you want to speak to me about . . .?"

"One who is called Quintero, and who is now a Villa guerrilla. A captain."

"He has a reputation, this Quintero. What do you wish to know?"

"Where he can be found."

"More men run from Quintero than seek to find him."

"I seek him."

"Word has come to us that the army of the United States has invaded us," Gómez said, "seeking Pancho Villa. But you do not seek Villa?"

"Only Quintero."

"It is unknown where either is. When the Americans invaded, both disappeared."

"What is this reputation of Quintero's of which you speak?"

Gómez said, "Did you know of Rodolfo Fierro, the one who was called by some El Carnicero, 'the Butcher'?"

"Who didn't?" Matt said. "He joined with Villa after I left, but every American read of his exploits in the newspapers. The newspapers in the United States called him Villa's Butcher."

"*Sí*. El Carnicero."

"We read that he personally executed by pistol three hundred Orozquistas in one afternoon, pausing only to massage a bruised trigger finger."

"Ay!" Gómez said. "That was a story! I heard it many times repeated in this cantina. How Fierro made each prisoner run for an adobe wall, then shot him dead before he could escape over it. Three hundred prisoners and three hundred rounds for his *pistolas* and he never missed. He had an orderly loading his guns, and his hands swelled from the recoil."

"I heard," Matt said.

"Well," Gomez said, "if you know about Fierro—he died last October, you know, drowned caught in some quicksand while fording a river on the way to fight at Agua Prieta—well, if you know about Rodolfo Fierro, you know about Captain Rodolfo Quintero. He is cast in the same mold. And equally vain of his reputation as a killer. And that is what they call Quintero. El Matador. 'The Killer.'"

"I am going to kill him."

"You? Why?"

Matt was silent.

Juanita said softly, "It is a matter of vengeance, Rafael. That is why Mateo seeks Quintero."

"Is this true?" Gómez said. He looked with new interest at Matt. "Tell me more of this," he said to the girl.

Juanita told him.

When she had finished, Gómez stared at Matt. He said, "I do not understand how you can hope to beat him. Twice you have encountered Quintero and twice he has wounded you. Why would a third time be better?"

"I only ask to find him."

"But why?"

"It is something I have to do."

"Because your woman asked you to? Surely, dying as she was, her judgment was impaired. She would not send you to your own death, had she realized—"

"I only ask to find him," Matt said again.

"Well," Gómez said, "I would help you if I could. But at the present, I know nothing. Nothing except that I do not think Quintero has passed through Parral."

"He passed through Galeana. And Namiquipa. And Bachíniva," Matt said. "This we learned on the way here."

"Your last word of him was in Bachíniva?"

"Yes."

"Hombre, Bachíniva is a distance of 150 miles. Quintero could be anywhere."

"Then I must find him."

"How?"

Matt shrugged.

"Let me suggest something," the *cantinero* said. "I have heard that Quintero owns a ranch over in the state of Durango. It is possible, now that the Americans have come, that he will take refuge there for a while."

"I must go there, then."

"I would not advise you to try it. It is a hard way. You have to cross the cursed Mapimí Desert to get there."

"I can cross a desert."

"Perhaps. But what happens when you get there? They say he keeps his ranch like a fort. He has a guard of his men on watch when he is there. Would you bait a bear in his own den?"

"If it is necessary."

"It would do no good. Besides, if he has not come through Parral, he will not be there. Mateo, you have already lost twice to him when he had the advantage over you. You have to find a way when the odds will be at least even."

"What, then, do you suggest?"

"Wait. Wait here in Parral. In this cantina I hear much. A cantina is a headquarters for news. What I hear is not always true, of course. But I will listen."

Juanita said, "Listen to him, Mateo. There is reason in what he says."

"And while I wait?" Matt said.

"Your *soldadera* is welcome back to her job here," Gómez said.

"And I have a small place to live, only a street away," Juanita said. "You will live there with me, Mateo, no? At least until your thigh is fully healed. It is only a short way to my house. But first we must take the horses to where they will be cared for."

They mounted, and Matt followed her as she led the way to the edge of the town and some livery stables with a corral next to a meadow.

The hostler was young and strongly built. He grinned at Juanita when he saw her and said, "Welcome to your home again, *chica*."

"It is good to be back," Juanita said. "I will board both horses now."

The stabler said, "Of course, *chica*. Your credit is always good with me." He was looking at Matt as he said it.

Matt stared at him but said nothing.

When they walked away, Matt said, "I did not like the way he called you *chica*."

"Many call me *chica* in this town," Juanita said. "I am a cantina girl, remember?"

Later she lay stretched out on her bed resting and looked up at him. "You are not yet healed, I can see that," she said. "The thigh is healing, but not the heart."

"I don't want to talk about it," he said. He went to the

shutters of a window in the mud-walled room and opened
them and looked out. He could see nothing except the
blank adobe wall of the hut next door. The afternoon sun had
already passed around so that the wall was shaded by the
hut of Juanita's.

"I am sorry if I bother you."

Suddenly he had to get away from her. It was as if Molly
could see him there with her. "I'm going to look around the
town," he said.

She got up and began to dress.

He turned from the window and looked at her. It seemed
to him that she was always there in front of him, showing
him her body.

What the hell is wrong with me? he thought.

"I will be at the cantina," she said resignedly. "Gómez
expects me there."

"You are fond of this gringo," Gómez said.

"Yes, Rafael," she said. "But it is more than a fondness."

"It goes back to when you were his *soldadera*, then?"

"Four years I thought about him and wondered where
he was. And one day I am washing clothes in the river at
Cobán and he falls from the sky, wounded, at my feet. Well,
not from the sky exactly. He fell from a sorrel horse."

"Unbelievable," Gómez said.

"This time the unbelievable happened. This time it
must mean something," she said.

"It seems so."

"You will help him find Quintero?"

Gómez shook his head. "If you love him, no."

"That is not the way he wants it."

"And what is the way *you* want it?"

"I do not know." She looked fully into Gómez's face. "I
love him. I do not want him killed. Still, until he does this
thing he can never forget his *gringa*."

"This, then, is a thing that comes between you?"

A flush came into her face, but she said, "I will say it—he can not be a whole man again until he avenges her."

"Christ!" Gómez said. "What a situation!"

CHAPTER 8

SHE was preparing a meal for them at her hut.

Matt said, "Working in the cantina, have you heard anything?"

"Nothing about Quintero. But there was a big battle at Guerrero, it is said. The Americans caught up with Villa there."

"Guerrero?"

"Southwest of Bachíniva, into the Sierra Madre. Sixty kilometers or more as the crow flies."

"The Americans? What units were involved?"

"I do not know the units. The information is sketchy," Juanita said. "It seems that Villa took Guerrero from a garrison of *federales* at dawn on the twenty-eighth of March. But the Americans heard of this in Bachíniva and rode all night through the mountains with a big force of cavalry and beat him badly at dawn of the twenty-ninth. Many Villistas were killed, it is said. It is said that Villa himself was wounded."

"And Quintero? Was Quintero there?"

"It is not known. If he was, I hope he was one who was killed."

"And I hope not," Matt said.

She looked at him sadly. "Ay, Mateo!" she said.

The five men came down the dusty street, riding abreast so that they took up its entire width. The one in the center sat tall in his saddle, his gaunt face set with fatigue but his wide shoulders erect.

"I could do with a drink, *mi capitán,*" one said, one who wore the black armband of mourning.

"We will have a drink," the tall one said. "Here at the Chihuahueño. I know the cantinero here." He gestured and they turned in at the cantina.

Inside, Gómez had just picked up a towel to wipe over his empty bar when he heard them. He looked out of the window and recognized Quintero and the towel fell out of his hand.

They came in and Quintero said, "Tequila for all."

"Of course," Gómez said, *"mi capitán."*

"So. You remember me, eh, *cantinero?"*

Gómez placed a bottle and glasses very carefully on the bar. He started to pour a tequila for Quintero, but Quintero shoved away his hand and took the bottle himself and poured his own. He pushed the bottle down to the next man then.

"One never forgets Captain Quintero," Gómez said. "All have heard of his exploits."

Quintero lifted his tequila and tossed it down. Then he said, "I have forgotten how you are called."

"Gómez. I call myself Gómez."

"Ah, Gómez. Well, Gómez, I will ask you a question."

"Sí, mi capitán."

"Have you seen a big gringo, wearing the uniform of a *norteamericano* sergeant, come to Parral?"

"Wearing the uniform of an American sergeant, you say? No, I have not seen such a gringo."

One of his men said, "Ay! After Guerrero I have seen enough gringos for a while." He reached for the bottle.

The one wearing the black armband said, "I have not. There is one gringo I would yet want to meet."

Gómez said, "We have heard briefly of Guerrero. You, then, were there?"

"We were there," the first man said. "We lost sixty killed and as many wounded. And *el general* himself took one in the knee."

Without looking at him Quintero said, "Shut your mouth!"

The man said, "I am sorry, *mi capitán*."

Quintero said to Gómez, "You are certain you did not see the gringo sergeant I described? We heard of his passing through Cienégita."

"Cienégita, perhaps, *mi capitán*. But certainly not here. But if I should know of such a one, I will tell you."

"I do not wait," Quintero said. "You are telling the truth, of course? You know what it would mean to lie to Quintero?"

"I know what it would mean, *mi capitán*. Definitely."

"It is well that you have considered this," Quintero said. He was staring at him closely.

"I have considered it, you can be certain," Gómez said. "I have not reached the age of forty by being stupid. But might I ask, *mi capitán*, where you journey to?"

Quintero downed another tequila, then set his glass hard on the bar. "You just said you were not stupid," he said.

The one with the loose tongue said, "We go to Mapimí. We have had enough of the gringos."

"Except one," the one with the armband said.

"*Cállase, todos!*" Quintero said angrily. "All of you shut up! Your tongues wag like those of women."

"Sorry, *mi capitán*. It is the tequila after a long thirst."

Quintero shoved the bottle back across the bar to Gómez. "Serve no more to these *bocones*, these bigmouths. If I was not short of men, I would put a pistol into the big mouth of each and blow their tongues out through their necks."

The one with the biggest mouth said, "But you will need us for your plans in Mapimí. Is it not true, *mi capitán*?"

"Enough!" Quintero said. "*Vámonos!* Now we ride some more."

Gómez sat at one of his tables in the empty cantina. Twice he wiped the sweat from his face with the bar towel he held in his hand. He sat as if his legs were too weak for him to get up. He kept looking at the door, hoping Quintero was gone for good.

Matt entered and Gómez gave a convulsive jerk.

"*Hola*, Rafael," Matt said. "What is wrong, hombre? *Qué pasó?*"

The *cantinero* got up and went to the bar. "Nothing is wrong with me," he said, over his shoulder. "But I am going to have a drink. Will you have one with me?"

"A pulque, then. *Gracias*."

Gómez poured the pulque for Matt, then said, "Something stronger for me," and reached for the bottle of tequila from which he had served Quintero, which was his best brand. He tossed the drink off fast while Matt sipped at his. He poured himself another. When he could feel both drinks in his belly he felt better, and he said, "You appear tired, Mateo."

"I spend the days walking the streets of Parral asking people what they know about Quintero. They are beginning to take me for a loco."

"And what do they tell you?"

"They tell me that he is *muy macho* and has big balls. They do not tell me where he is."

"I have heard he was at Guerrero."

"That *is* news!"

"And Villa was shot in the knee there."

"Where are they now?"

"Who knows? But me, I have my own idea where Villa is—when he is in trouble, he heads back into Durango. He is not a true *chihuahueño*, you know—only by adoption. He was born in Las Nieves, in Durango."

"And Quintero?"

"He was born in hell."

"I mean, where is he now?"

"If I knew, I would tell you."

"But where do you think he is?"

Gómez looked at Matt and did not answer at once. He seemed to be making a hard decision. Then he dropped his eyes to the bar and said, "I have no idea."

Juanita said to Gómez, "But when did you see him?"

"Mateo?"

"Not Mateo! I know Mateo was here earlier."

"Christ on the cross! it was close!" Gómez said. "I mean, Mateo showing up here not ten minutes after."

"That close?"

"That close," the *cantinero* said. "I was just opening for business and I looked outside and there comes Quintero riding down the street, him and the four others."

She said, "Mateo will be furious that you did not tell him of this."

Gómez looked worried. "I know it. At first I hesitated to send him word. Then, when he came here, I hesitated further. And then I knew I would not tell him."

"I understand," Juanita said. "But Mateo will not."

"You understand that if I told him it would be signing his death warrant. The five against one, here in the streets of Parral."

She nodded. "He has already met the five."

"This time he would not be so lucky. They would shoot him down like a stray dog."

"I will have to tell him," Juanita said. "But I will wait until they are well gone."

Gómez shook his head. "Do not do it. There is nothing to gain by telling him. Wait until Quintero is in Mapimí. I will tell him then, myself. When it is too far for him to do anything rash."

"I am torn."

"Do you love this gringo?"

"I love him much. I told you before."

"Then do not tell him about Quintero."

Matt walked the streets of Parral as he had been doing these several days. The people of the town had come to accept him as a familiar sight. Many thought he was a little loco, but they treated him with a grave courtesy, possibly because of this, and also because for a gringo he spoke good Spanish. His questions made them nervous, though, and they weren't certain he wasn't a spy for the American forces that were scattered over the north half of Chihuahua looking for Villa. Everybody except the Americans, of course, knew Villa was over in the state of Durango.

What made them nervous most of all was that Matt's questions were about Quintero. The Matador himself. The Killer who tried to walk in the big footprints of Rodolfo Fierro, the Butcher, who, thank God! was now buried deep somewhere in quicksand.

Even when they learned the gringo was a sergeant deserter from his own army and certainly not a spy, they still worried when he asked about Quintero. It wasn't a good thing to talk about the Killer. Your words might reach his ears distorted and give offense, and if that happened you could live in fright for the rest of your short life.

On this day Matt suddenly noticed that things seemed different. He began to observe that when he walked down one side of the street, people crossed to the opposite side. He thought, I have bothered them too often with my questions. I must learn to be less abrupt. I must learn to just listen and not to ask. He wondered himself if he wasn't getting a little loco in his frustration. People had now taken to addressing him as Sergeant Gringo, so he guessed he might have let slip why he asked about Quintero. They might have learned about Molly and the terrible night at Gunlock.

Perhaps Gómez had let the story out. You could never be sure about a *cantinero*. They all liked to talk too much, even those who pretended to be closemouthed.

Maybe he had done just that himself. The days had gone on and on and he was getting no closer to Quintero. He had to meet with Quintero before the rest of his life could begin. Maybe he wouldn't have a chance to start over after meeting Quintero. If so, that was the way it had to be.

Just then a man he knew crossed the street to avoid him. The man had been friendly to him before, more friendly perhaps than most.

He waited until he was across the street and then Matt cut across himself. There was no way the other could cross again without looking foolish. The man saw that, and as he came toward Matt he wore a frustrated look.

"*Hola, amigo,*" Matt said.

"*Buenos días,* Sergeant Gringo." The man nodded and tried to pass.

Matt reached out and touched his sleeve. "Wait, please. A thing gives me much conern."

"What thing, *sargento?*"

"That all avoid me today. Even you, amigo."

"I, Sergeant?"

"*Sí,* you. And all the others."

The man looked at him. Then he looked over his shoulder, and then up and down the street carefully. "It is clear that you have not heard," he said.

"Heard what, amigo?"

The man cleared his throat as if it were hard for him to speak. "You have asked about Captain Quintero several times," he said.

"That is a fact."

"He rode through Parral this morning. We cross the street because we are not certain he has gone. Well, we are certain, but even so—"

"Quintero here? In Parral?"

"*Sí*, Sergeant. Many saw and recognized him."

"At what time?"

"He rode through about ten," the man said. "Then he rode south. Let us hope he continues."

"He did not stop?"

"Only briefly. At the place of Gómez."

Matt stopped by Juanita's hut and got her revolver and stuck it in his belt. He got the Krag-Jorgensen carbine too. Then he went to the cantina.

There was a crowd in there now, and they were all talking. When he went in, the talking stopped. Gómez stood behind the bar. He met Matt's stare and then his eyes dropped. Matt strode toward him, his cavalry boots sounding hard against the packed-mud floor.

"Quintero was here?"

"You have only to listen to these fools to know," Gómez said. "They are talking of nothing else. How can I deny it?"

"He was here before I spoke with you this morning."

"I do not deny that, either."

"Why did you not tell me, then?"

"Why? To save your life, amigo. They were five, again."

"Is my life so valuable to you?"

"Not to me, Mateo. But to Juanita it is."

"Does she know about this?"

"She knows now. She did not earlier."

"But she did not come to tell me," Matt said. He looked around the cantina and saw that all were watching him. He turned and started for the door.

"*A dónde vas*, Mateo?"

"To get my horse," he said.

He walked fast toward the livery stable. He did not see the stableman and so he took a reata off a peg in a tack room and went out into the meadow where the sorrel grazed. The horse was well rested and lively now, and Matt cursed at the trouble he had catching it. When he finally got it saddled, he rammed the Krag-Jorgensen into the scabbard and swung up, ready to ride away.

The young stableman appeared suddenly and stopped him by grabbing hold of the bridle. "*Un momento,*" he said. "There is money owing for the horse's care. I would not trouble you but—"

"Don't, then."

"—You might not come back from where you are going."

"Where do you think I am going?"

"I would guess, Sergeant Gringo, that you take to the trail of Quintero," the stableman said. "If so, it is only good business that I ask you to pay now."

Matt pondered this. "All right," he said. "I have no money to pay, but take this." He took the revolver from his belt and held it butt first toward the hostler.

The stableman looked into his face. "You would ride after Quintero without a gun?"

"I have a carbine," Matt said and slapped the saddle scabbard.

"No, *sargento,*" the stableman said. "If you go after Quintero, take the pistol too." He pushed the gun back toward Matt. "I will take a chance on the money."

Matt nodded and turned the sorrel south onto the main road.

He began to think then, and to wonder what he would do if he caught up to Quintero and four of his men. He had done that before, and where had it got him?

He could remain hidden and snipe and possibly kill them that way. Quintero, anyway.

But the thought of that did not excite him. Quintero would never know why he died. He would never know that he died because of what he did to Molly.

It was necessary to Matt that he know, for his own sake and for Molly's. That was the way she would have wanted it.

Just ahead, near the edge of Parral, he could see the curved structure of the town's bullfight arena, the *plaza de toros*. It was deserted now, but on certain afternoons during the season, when the Revolution wasn't too close, it would be crowded and alive with excitement.

The road passed close to the entrance, and he could see above the sandy arena the tiers of seats where the crowds came at four o'clock on those afternoons to shout *"Olé!"* at the matadors if they killed successfully, to hurl insults and bottles if they did not.

Then suddenly he thought to himself, I wonder if they would come to see a man kill a *man?*

He reined up the sorrel and sat thinking. The idea began to grow. He felt an excitement begin.

He turned and rode back toward the town.

A gunfight. Just me and Quintero. Here in the bullring in Parral.

A killer like Quintero, so vain about his reputation, could he refuse a challenge like that?

CHAPTER 9

THE punitive expedition into Mexico was stalled.

In a single week after the border raids it had been organized, given to the command of Brigadier General "Black Jack" Pershing, and thrown in rage into Chihuahua.

But now, three weeks after that, it had lost its drive.

The main reason for this was simple. The Villistas had disappeared.

Pershing's orders sounded simple enough in the beginning: "The Expedition has the sole object of capturing Pancho Villa and preventing any further raids by his bands ... with scrupulous regard to the sovereignty of Mexico."

The "sovereignty of Mexico" business was another reason the expedition was stalled. Carranza, playing for political sympathy on the patriotism of the Mexican people, had suddenly made it a big issue. He now refused to let Pershing use the Mexican Northwest Rail Line to bring supplies from El Paso to his extended troops.

These hungry troops were scattered halfway down Chihuahua and had to requisition food from the Mexicans. And the latter, Villista and Carrancista sympathizers alike, aroused by Carranza's anti-American rhetoric, were reluctant suppliers. Carranza, the politician, had united the sentiments of both factions against the expeditionary force.

Pershing had a lot of mouths to feed. In the week he'd had to mobilize his command, he'd grabbed what was available near the border. Primarily the 7th, 10th, 11th, and

13th cavalries. He also had two mountain gun batteries of four guns each — 2.95-inch howitzers with an effective range of three miles. It took four mules to carry one of these guns disassembled, plus six mules for the ammunition. He also had the 6th and the 16th infantry regiments for use as guards along the tortuous, rutted supply road from Columbus, forming a long line of groaning lorries and wagons.

In short, Black Jack Pershing had forty-eight hundred men and four thousand horses and mules in a hostile land, all scantily provisioned.

But Black Jack was used to hostile country. As a lieutenant he had campaigned against Geronimo in Arizona.

Now, when he was hard-pressed to feed his men and had no target of opportunity on which to use them, the top command sent him reinforcements: another mountain gun battery, a battalion of the 24th Infantry and a squadron of the 5th Cavalry.

He also had Holcomb's provisional squadron of the 12th, now bivouacked at Bachíniva.

Major Holcomb was exultant. The weeks of waiting at Bachíniva had ended suddenly with a dispatch from Pershing, who was now headquartered at Namiquipa, forty miles to the north.

Holcomb called in his officers and the scout, Lacy. Captain Walker, who had rejoined the squadron as soon as his shoulder wound allowed, and Lieutenant Darwin both noted the elation that showed through the major's hard-bitten expression.

"Gentlemen," Holcomb said, "we're going to see some action at last. Movement, anyway. It seems we've been stuck in this goddam hole for months instead of weeks. Well, here are orders to move." He held up the Pershing dispatch. "It appears that the other units have been getting most of some mighty scarce action, but *this* could be interesting."

"They've located Villa?" Walker said.

Holcomb scowled. "No. We're not *that* lucky. Not yet. But you know that we've got two enemies down here. Villa is one, of course—that is, if anybody ever finds him or his bandits again. Our other enemy, it appears, is Carranza and his federal troops."

Lieutenant Darwin said, "Sir, I thought he'd welcome our help in going after Villa."

Holcomb snorted. "You can't tell what any of these double-dealing politicians will do. In the beginning he wanted to get rid of Villa, of course. When we didn't catch him right away, he got some grumble from the rest of the Mexicans. To take the sting out of that, the two-faced sonofabitch decided to pretend he'd never given us permission to enter the country. He's using our presence here for a smoke screen, appealing to national pride, claiming we invaded Mexico against his wishes. He may even try using the *federales* to drive us out of Chihuahua. That would stick a big feather in his sombrero."

"Is this the official belief of the War Department, Major?" Captain Walker said.

"Who knows? It's my belief, anyway. Recent developments seem to be bearing me out."

"Something new, sir?" Walker said.

Again, Holcomb picked up the dispatch from Pershing and waved it. "The general is worried about the movement of federal troops out of Saltillo in recent days. His information has it that fifteen thousand of them were there a couple of weeks ago. Now it appears that some have moved out toward San Isabel. They're coming this way and getting close."

"And your orders, Major?" Walker said.

Holcomb took the dispatch and read directly from it. "'You will take your troops and reconnoiter in the direction of San Isabel and obtain as much information as you can regarding the forces there. This is a reconnaisance only, and you will not be expected to fight. Avoid a fight if possible. Do not allow yourself to be surprised by superior numbers. But if wantonly attacked, use your judgment as to what you should do.'"

Walker said, "It sounds routine enough. I notice he says to avoid a fight."

Holcomb stared at him. "Routine? Captain, where is your imagination? This is what we've been waiting for. We may get a chance to make some history."

The squadron of the 12th rode out south to the drab little town of Agua Caliente, a spattering of mud spots stuck to the monotonous earth. They turned eastward there, following the wind of the Mexican Northwestern tracks through the hills. Late on the second day they broke out on a sparsely grassed plain and saw a ranch in the distance.

Lacy said, "That's the San Simeon ranch, Major. American owned and operated. I know the foreman there. Leastwise I did a couple of years back. Might be he can give us some information."

They approached the sprawl of the ranch buildings, built near a cottonwood-lined creek.

"We'll bivouac here," Holcomb said, "by the creek."

"Better let me look for McKay, the foreman I mentioned," Lacy said. "Ain't manners to just squat on a ranch property down here without asking permission."

"We're the U.S. Army," Holcomb said. "Go find the goddam foreman, if you like, but here's where we're making camp, regardless."

Lacy shrugged. "It's your decision."

He didn't have to look for McKay. The man spotted them from the ranch house and came racing his horse across the compound. Lacy rode out to intercept him.

McKay was big and bluff and middle-aged, with a face that the years had sunburned without tanning. He had a frown that was more perplexed than angry. When he recognized Lacy, his expression eased. "Lacy!" He rode close and took Lacy's extended hand and pumped it vigorously. Then he said, "But what the hell is going on here?"

Lacy said, "I'm scouting for a cavalry squadron. You know about the expedition, don't you?"

"Of course. Everybody in Mexico knows about it. We've not seen any of it this far east, though."

"No, I reckon not. Well, the major's got orders to reconnoiter the area. Hope it's all right to stay here overnight?"

"For the American army? Hell, yes!" McKay said. "Been more courteous for somebody to ask first, though."

"Ain't the major's way," Lacy said.

"Reckon not. Well, let's meet him."

They rode over to where Holcomb was watching his men set up camp. They dismounted and McKay held out his hand. "Major," he said.

Holcomb took it, gripping hard as he looked up at the much bigger man.

McKay suppressed a grin as he felt the pressure against his powerful but relaxed knuckles. He wondered fleetingly what it was that drove some men to make a feat of strength out of what should be a gesture of friendship. Just for kicks he tightened his own big grip and saw the pain show in the major's face before he hid it. When he let go, the major pulled his hand back quickly and shoved it into his pants pocket.

"This is McKay," Lacy said belatedly.

"You are the foreman here, I understand," Holcomb said. "Any information you can give us about the military situation in the area?"

"Is the army still trying to find Villa, Major?"

"Do you know where he is?"

"Nobody seems to know where he is."

Lacy said, "What we're here for is to find out what the *federales* are doing."

McKay said, "I can tell you this: Four hundred of them

camped right where you're camping a week ago. Under the
command of Colonel Brito."

"Where are they now?"

"Moved back nine miles east. Little town there called
Corrales. Halfway to San Isabel, more or less. Brito's taken
over one of the adobes there for his headquarters."

Holcomb seemed to welcome this information. "He's between us and San Isabel, then?"

"That's right, Major."

"My orders," Holcomb said, "are to reconnoiter the area
of San Isabel."

"Well, now," McKay said, "I don't know how kindly
Brito will take to that. You know there's a lot of resentment
lately about Americans busting into the country and—"

"What do you mean, busting in?"

"Manner of speaking," McKay said easily. "Way most
Mexicans see it, I reckon. Anyway, you'll find Colonel
Brito a pretty reasonable man—if you don't cross him."

Holcomb said testily, "I'm not concerned about Brito's
feelings."

McKay looked at Lacy, who avoided his glance, then
looked back at Holcomb. "Like I just said, Major—Colonel
Brito is a pretty reasonable man—if you don't cross him."

"My orders are to reconnoiter the area of San Isabel,"
Holcomb said again. "And by God, I intend to do just that."

McKay said calmly, "Could be there'll be no problem,
Major. Hell, there is a road goes south around the town and
meets the San Isabel road beyond. All you might have to do
is detour that way. The terrain is hilly, but it ain't more
than five miles farther than going straight through the
town."

"We'll see," Holcomb said shortly. "We'll be moving out
in the morning. Before dawn."

McKay looked thoughtful. He said, "I know Colonel
Brito. Might be I should go along."

At 0400 hours the squadron of the 12th was mounted and

ready, formed a column of fours, and started down the dirt road that led from the San Simeon to Corrales.

At 0530 they reached another creek a mile from the town and watered their horses. Holcomb and his officers studied the ground ahead of them. The buildings of Corrales were partly hidden by cottonwoods and an orchard that lined a deep irrigation ditch that cut in front of the town itself. Between the squadron position and the irrigation ditch there were six hundred yards of open ground, totally without cover.

Lacy borrowed Holcomb's field glasses and looked along the line of trees. He said, "They've spotted us, Major."

"So?"

"I don't like it. They got troops coming out of the town, going into position among them cottonwoods." He swept the terrain with the glasses. "Hell, they got men already in that ditch."

McKay, the San Simeon foreman, said, "Was me, Major, I'd ask Brito before I did anything rash."

"Are you a military man, McKay?"

"No," McKay said. "But I understand Mexicans. I understand *macho*."

"*Macho?*"

"Something peculiar to the Mexican race, Major. I don't know how to explain it exactly. Kind of a pride. More than that. Courage. Manliness. Guts. It's what makes a Mexican man tick."

"So?"

"All I know, Major, is that if you step on a Mexican's *machismo,* you better be ready to fight to the death."

"Bullshit!" Holcomb said.

Lacy said anxiously, "Sure wouldn't hurt none to send that Mex colonel a request, asking permission to enter. Hell, Major, it'd just be an asking from one officer to another."

"They know me," McKay said. "I'd be glad to take the request in."

Holcomb said grudgingly, "All right. But I'm not going to beg from that Mexican."

He seemed to touch a nerve in McKay. The ranch foreman turned to face him. "You got a lot to learn about a Mexican's guts," he said.

McKay rode out on the open ground and the *federales* in the trees let him come. He disappeared into the grove. Fifteen minutes passed and he rode back into sight and returned to where the squadron waited. He said, "Colonel Brito sends his regrets. But he cannot let you pass through the town. He has orders from higher up."

"I don't believe that. He's lying," Holcomb said. He said to Captain Walker, "Mount the troops. We're moving up. I'm going to call his bluff."

McKay said, "Bad business. Brito isn't a man to bluff."

Walker hesitated, and Holcomb said, "You heard my order."

The squadron mounted and rode slowly forward, Holcomb out in front. Halfway to the trees he halted, seeing a *federale* riding toward them carrying a white flag.

"I knew I'd back the bastard down," Holcomb said.

The *federale* stopped and dismounted. He saluted, then held out a piece of paper. Holcomb looked at it, then scowled. "Lacy, do you read Mexican?"

"*I* can," McKay said. "Read Spanish, that is."

Holcomb handed him the note.

McKay scanned it, then said, "Colonel Brito invites you to enter Corrales with a few of your men — for a conference."

"Smells like a trap to me," Holcomb said. "Refuse the offer."

McKay reluctantly handed the order back to the messenger.

Holcomb said to Walker, "Move up another hundred yards. Skirmish formation!"

The troops moved up as the messenger hurried in front of them to return to his own lines.

Immediately four officers appeared, one carrying another flag of truce.

McKay said, "That's Brito in the lead. It appears he wants to discuss this with you."

Colonel Brito and his officers halted precisely halfway.

"Major," Lacy said, "you got to meet him there."

"All right." Holcomb rode forward, both Lacy and McKay beside him. Lieutenant Darwin produced a white cloth from somewhere and rode with them, holding the rag aloft.

The two commanders sat in their saddles eyeing each other.

Colonel Brito spoke first. His voice was quiet and courteous, but emphatic.

McKay interpreted. "The colonel gives his regards. But he repeats: he cannot allow you to move through Corrales."

"Tell him that I have orders to go to San Isabel."

McKay repeated the message.

Colonel Brito smiled. He talked rapidly, in an easy voice. When he finished, he smiled again.

McKay said, "Colonel Brito says his orders do not refuse you permission to go around Corrales to get to San Isabel. They only refuse you permission to go through Corrales."

"What the hell difference does it make, then, if I go through?"

"A matter of *macho*, Major. And I might ask, what the hell difference does it make, then, if you go around?"

"Tell him I'm going through the town. I'm not sidetracking for any Mexican."

Colonel Brito must have understood some of it. He stopped smiling and his face took on a bitter look. When he spoke again his words were flat and hard.

Lacy spoke up. "Major, he says if you insist on going through the town you will do so only over the bodies of dead government soldiers—and Americans too."

"What the hell is the sense?" McKay said. "Go around, Major. Hell, you got two hundred yards of open ground between the *federales* and you. They got the advantage all on their side."

Colonel Brito spoke a sharp question.

"He wants to know your answer."

"Tell him he already knows it," Holcomb said. He turned his horse and rode back to the skirmish line, leaving the others to follow.

McKay remained where he was for a moment, facing Colonel Brito. He met Brito's eyes and shook his head slowly.

A sadness came into Brito's face. Then, abruptly, he raised a quirt in a half salute and wheeled away.

Captain Walker met Holcomb as he came back. "What now, sir?"

"Prepare for a mounted charge."

"They'll cut us down like a scythe."

"I won't let that bastard stop me."

"Wouldn't he let us go around Corrales?"

"Captain," Holcomb said tightly, "I intend to go through Corrales. Prepare to charge."

"But sir—"

"Give the order, mister."

Captain Walker called it out.

Lieutenant Darwin swore under his breath. Behind him he could hear some of his own troopers swearing aloud. A sergeant's voice reached him: "Christ, sir, this is—"

Holcomb's voice sounded. "Charge!" He started in a run for the tree-lined ditch.

The squadron raced in line behind him.

The *federale* rifles opened up. Troopers and horses went down.

Holcomb went through the curtain of lead without a scratch. He reached the irrigation ditch and plunged his horse into it, firing his pistol point-blank into the Mexicans deployed there. There were men of the 12th right behind him and on either side doing the same.

The Mexicans broke, tried to scramble up the far bank on foot, the troopers riding them down as the horses surged upward.

And then more fire came from the orchard beyond. Holcomb just reached the top of the bank when a bullet slammed into him, knocked him out of his saddle. He landed hard on the bank and rolled down and his hat came off and his gray head smashed against a jutting rock and he didn't move again.

Captain Walker saw this and yelled for the troopers to fall back into the ditch and take cover.

The fire from the orchard was murderous. The troopers fell back, some knocked there by bullets.

And then a troop of Mexican cavalry rode in a large, sweeping circle to the north and took up position along the creek where the 12th had earlier watered their horses.

"They've got us in a cross fire now," Darwin said.

Walker looked down to where Holcomb lay unconscious, blood running from a deep gash in his temple. Darwin had opened the major's shirt to expose another long furrow along his ribs where a bullet had gouged him to the bone. It was bleeding badly.

"He's losing a lot of blood, sir."

"Let the bastard bleed," Walker said. He looked over toward the creek and saw Lacy and McKay, who had not taken part in the charge, riding out from the Mexican cavalry position. "Hold your fire!" he yelled to the troopers in the ditch.

The two cowboys rode closer. Lacy yelled, "Major?"

Walker hollered back. "He's out of it."

"I'm coming in to talk to you."

"Come ahead."

A moment later the two cowboys slid down into the ditch. Lacy spotted the major lying still beside the rock he'd struck his head against. "Looks like you're in command now, Captain."

"Only good thing that's happened here today," McKay said. "I sure hope you got more brains than that oak-leafed *pendejo*. Is he dead?"

"Knocked out, I think," Darwin said. "He's still breathing."

"Too bad," McKay said. "Captain, none of this was Brito's wanting. He wants you to know that. He says the *federales* are not at war with the United States. They only want to let the Americans know they are still in charge of the country. So he's willing to let you pull out, provided you leave Corrales."

"His offer to go around to the San Isabel road still hold?"

"No. He withdraws that offer. You'll have to pull back. You can take your dead and wounded to the San Simeon. From there you got to return to Bachíniva. You agree to this and he will let you go in peace. He says enough men have died on both sides."

Captain Walker said, "I understand. I agree to his terms."

Darwin said, "What about the major? If he regains consciousness . . ."

Walker looked over to Holcomb's inert figure. His face grew bitter and determined. "Lieutenant, I can't stand to see the major suffer. I happen to have some morphine in a medical kit. Do you suppose a shot of it would ease his pain and possibly put him to sleep?"

"It would be worth a try, sir," Darwin said.

Luckily, the major had bled enough that, combined with the sedative, he did not reach consciousness on the way to the San Simeon. There McKay agreed to sell them wagons and mules for the wounded. The dead were buried in the ranch cemetery. Twelve men had been killed and ten wounded.

They never knew how many Mexicans died at Corrales.

McKay summed it up as the brief burial service conducted by Walker ended. "They all died for nothing," he said bitterly. "They all died, on both sides, because that bastard major stepped on a Mexican's *machismo*."

They were well on the way back toward Agua Caliente before Holcomb finally came around. He'd lost a lot of blood, but none of his feisty spirit. As soon as he could talk he tied into Captain Walker for surrendering to Brito's terms.

Walker said stubbornly, "You were out of it, sir, and it was my decision to make. I made what I judged to be the correct one under the circumstances."

"I hate to think that colonel beat us," Holcomb said. "Can you imagine that stupid bastard—letting this *macho* business influence his decisions?"

Walker ignored the question. "We accomplished what we set out to do. We found out there are Carrancistas in strength in the area."

"Yeah," Holcomb said. His voice suddenly sounded tired. "You know, Walker, I've been wounded before. One thing bothers me about this time—why it took me so long to come around."

Walker exchanged glances with Lieutenant Darwin. Darwin said, "It must have been the blow on the head that did it, sir."

CHAPTER 10

"WELL," Gómez, the *cantinero*, said, "I will tell you what I know now."

They were sitting in Gómez's place, the Cantina Chihuahueño, Matt and the girl and Gómez.

"A man hears many rumors in a place like this," Gómez said. "Some true, some false. But after a while one grows a feel for separating the two. *Más o menos.* More or less."

Matt and Juanita waited.

"This, then, is what I know," Gómez said. "That Villa now recuperates in the state of Durango, as I suspected. That he is in a place of caves he has used before."

"I have heard of the place," Juanita said. "I have heard it said that the place is deep in the mountains near the Mapimí Desert."

"That, too, is what I heard," Gómez said.

"Could a gringo find his way there?"

"He would get no help from Mexicans, if that is what you mean. Even down there in the remotes of Durango, the people will have heard of the gringo invasion of our country."

Matt frowned. "You have a a feeling against gringos, too?"

Gómez shrugged. "I did not say that. I simply try to give you the flavor of the sentiment of our people. I will say it again: You will get only wrong information from those you question. Simply because you are *yanqui*." He grinned. "After all, to a Mexican, all gringos look alike."

"What do you suggest, then?"

Again Gómez shrugged. He looked at Juanita.

Juanita said, "I have discussed this with Rafael. There is only one way you will get to Villa: I must go with you."

"Why?"

"I am Mexican, and that will help. I have some idea of where the hideout of Villa is, and I have been once before over that mountain trail. It is another way to get to Mapimí. Shorter than the road around by way of Jiménez, which is east, then south. The mountain trail goes southwest, then east."

"If you could draw a map for me?"

She went on as if he hadn't spoken. "There are the mountains, of course, and beyond is the terrible desert. I hope the hideout is before the desert, but we cannot be sure. On that desert, if you have not been taken across before, you would die, Mateo. Believe me. I remember it from years back."

Gómez nodded. "Believe what she says, amigo. I have heard tales of the Mapimí Desert. I want to help you, Mateo, because you are a gringo I like. One who has fought for the Revolution, for Villa. That is a great thing in your favor—to have fought for Villa. It is said he never forgets neither his enemies nor his friends."

Matt said, "I am hunted by my own army. I cannot waste more time. I must have my chance at vengeance before I am taken by the military police or others."

"Then we must go at once," Juanita said. "Rafael, we have horses. Can you loan us the rent for a pack mule and for provisions?"

"How not?" Gómez said. "You are my friends, no?"

At first the way was easy. They followed the main road south, leading toward the city of Durango, which was more than two hundred miles into the center of the state. This part had been ground out of the mountainous terrain by the passage of centuries of traders and miners.

But on the morning of the third day, between Ocampo and Zarca, Juanita turned eastward off the road and onto a lesser one, hardly more than a horse trail.

This was high, dry country. The trail wound past peaks and ridges without trees except for occasional patches of juniper.

"You spoke of a desert," Matt said once.

"Believe me, Mateo, this is not it," Juanita said. "The desert is out there ahead somewhere. I do not remember exactly. It was long ago when I crossed it with others."

"The canteens are nearly empty and the horses have thirst."

"We will find water, Mateo."

"You relieve my mind considerably," Matt said.

In the midmorning of the fourth day they came to the sight of a lookout. Matt happened to look ahead as they wound the animals through a series of rocky ravines, and he saw the sombreroed figure on the skyline of a ridge.

"We are seen," he said.

"You are sure?"

"I am sure."

"Let us hope, Mateo, that it is one of Villa's men."

"My thought exactly," Matt said.

They entered a narrow way where a ravine became a barranca. There was a sharp curve in the barranca and they rounded it and came faceup against a pair of rifles pointing at them through the rocks.

"*Manos arriba!*"

They raised their hands quickly. Juanita called, "*Somos amigos!* Here we are friends."

A voice behind a rifle said, "Friends, eh? Of whom?"

"Villa," Matt said.

"Too bad," a second voice said, very deep for a Mexican. "We are Carrancistas here."

Both voices burst into laughter.

Matt felt suddenly cold.

The rifles moved forward, followed by their holders, two men in charro clothes. One of them stepped to Matt's side and took the Krag carbine from its scabbard. He moved over to Juanita and reached up and lifted the pistol from her holster. He stared up into her face. "Villa has pretty friends," he said. Then he looked over at Matt. He shook his head, "Well, not all are so." This was the one with the deep voice who spoke.

The other turned and walked up the barranca floor.

"*Sígalo,*" the deep-voiced one said. "Follow him."

A short distance ahead, their horses were tethered. They mounted up. "*Siga,*" the Mexican basso said again, and they rode on in the same order.

The barranca floor rose and flared until presently they were on the side of a low, broad peak with an escarpment on either side. The escarpments and the side of the peak were very rocky, but there were junipers growing, and here and there a stand of Jeffrey pine.

Matt said over his shoulder to the basso behind him, "There is water here?"

"*Sí. Un manantial.* A spring." The basso added, "Amigo." And laughed.

Me and my mouth, Matt thought. But hell, if they were Carrancistas they ought to be in *federale* uniform. Unless they were irregulars.

They reached a spot that had been leveled for a corral. The corral held a half-dozen horses. Just above and beyond was the mouth of a cave formed by a granite slab that jutted from the slope overhead.

Another man stood by the corral. He was dressed in tan clothes and had a peaked campaign hat like that of a cavalry trooper. He wore a revolver, slung low on his hip, and a belt filled with cartridges.

The Mexican in the lead rode up to him, dismounted, and said, "Visitors, *mi capitán.*"

"So I see."

"Something is wrong here," Matt said to Juanita, who was in front of him.

Her low-voiced reply seemed to have relief in it. "I do not think so."

The captain said, "Dismount."

The one with the deep voice waited until Matt and the girl were off their horses, then he swung down from his saddle. He said, "They claim to be friends of Villa, *mi capitán*."

"Is this true?" the captain said to Matt.

Matt was tempted to deny it.

While he hesitated the basso said, "I told him we were Carrancistas, *mi capitán*."

"Good," the captain said.

Juanita said, "It is true, Captain. We *are* friends. And friends of Villa's Dorados. 'The Golden Ones.'"

"Ah," the captain said. "You recognize my uniform, then." He looked at the girl with amused appreciation.

The deep-voiced Mexican laughed. "It was my joke, *mi capitán*."

The Dorado captain smiled. "And a good one, too," he said. He looked closely at Matt's face. "I judge so by the expression on the gringo's face."

"Some joke," Matt said tightly.

"Climb up there to the cave," the Dorado said.

It was a short, easy climb. Here and there crude steps had been scratched out of the rocky soil. They reached the broad mouth of the cave and Matt strained to see into the gloom.

He recognized the blocky figure at once, even though Villa limped as he shambled forward, leaning his weight on a crude cane.

"*Qué pasa?*" Villa said.

"They say they are friends of yours, *mi general*."

"Many say so," Villa said. "But how do I know?"

Juanita spoke before Matt could answer. "We fought for you and the Revolution at the first Juárez and after, *mi general*. Both of us."

"Both of you?"

"I was a *soldadera*," Juanita said.

"But him. He is gringo."

Matt said, "Yes, I am gringo. And so was Captain Sammie Dreben, *mi general*. There was that morning we fought in the streets of Juárez, throwing grenades we'd made the night before from tin cans stuffed with powder and dynamite and nails and screws."

"My Gringo Legion!" Villa said. "That Sammie Dreben! *Qué hombre! Qué soldado!* What a fighting man! All of you!" His full face, with the great brush of reddish black mustache, suddenly lost its animation and he seemed about to cry. "Why did you gringos turn against me, *muchacho?* Why did you do that to me at Agua Prieta?"

Matt remembered the stories he'd heard about Villa's emotional instability. His swings from high to low, impulses that could change him from compassion to cruelty, from cold-blooded butcher to a sobbing mourner for men slaughtered on the battlefields. Sometimes he would cry for men he had coldly ordered executed only moments before. No one could ever be sure of how to take Villa; in fact you could only be sure of two things about him: he always had courage, and his word was always good.

Matt said, "It was the politicos who turned against you, *mi general,* not the American people." He hesitated, then added, "Not until the raids on the border."

Villa shook his head. "That was a mistake, *muchacho*. I was angry about Agua Prieta or I never would have allowed them."

"It is because of that, *mi general,* that I have come to you."

"Well, speak, then."

"It is because of the raid on Gunlock that I come."

"Why?"

"I lost my wife there. And now I search for the one who raped and killed her—a Captain Quintero."

"Quintero?"

"He is here?"

Villa shook his head. "What are your intentions if you find him?"

"I wish to meet him in a gunfight. *Mano a mano.*"

"You have *huevos grandes, muchacho.* But Quintero is not here."

"Mateo—this is Mateo, *mi general*—" Juanita said, "he desires to challenge Quintero to a gunfight in the bullring in Parral."

Villa stared at her. "You joke, of course."

"No, *mi general.* Mateo has searched for Quintero since the raid. He has lost hope of finding him alone. Now he would dare Quintero to come out to meet him thus."

"In the *plaza de toros!* Your Mateo has the *huevos* of a bull himself. In Parral, eh?"

"*Sí, mi general,*" Matt said.

"Tell me, *muchacho,* are the *federales* now holding Parral?"

"No, *mi general.* Those who were there have been sent northward to garrison the towns nearer where the Americans are."

"And how far south are the Americans?"

"Bachíniva is what we hear," Matt said.

"Well," Villa said, "I have had it in my mind to visit Parral. The people like me there. But I have no troops with me. Only a handful of my loyal Dorados. My Golden Ones. I once had more than three hundred. Many are still on call, but I have sent them home until I recover."

"I am sorry to hear of your wound, *mi general.* You took a gringo bullet at Guerrero?"

"Not a gringo bullet. I was hit the day before the fight with the Americans. The morning I took Guerrero from the

Carrancistas. A bullet from an old Remington .44, American made but in the hands of a cursed *federale*. A big bullet that splintered my shin. But I am nearly healed now."

"The people of Parral, they still love you, *mi general*," Juanita said.

"Parral has always been a town for me," Villa said. "I would like to return. I have your word there are no American troops near there?"

"I do not know of any," Matt said. "And what about the matter of Quintero?"

"Ah, Quintero. It is a rare thing that you should ask, *muchacho*. For I have been thinking some of Quintero also. He came by here a time ago, but he continued on across the desert to a ranch he owns near Mapimí. To await orders from me, of course. At least, that is what he is supposed to be doing."

Villa paused, then went on: "But I have been hearing strange things about my Captain Quintero. Rumors that he is getting too big for his pants. Rumors that he has been plundering banks, extorting money from the common people, even selling beef to the *federales* on the sly. These are bad things which could turn the people against me, many knowing that he is one of my own men."

Matt said, "You will help me, then, *mi general?*"

Villa smiled. "*Muchacho*, let me tell you something. I recognized and remembered you when you came climbing up the trail there a few minutes ago."

"That you should remember a mere gringo *soldado!*" Matt said. "How is that, *mi general?*"

"I will tell you how. I remember you at the side of Captain Sammie Dreben, all right. And the business of the grenades that morning when we took Juárez. That was the first big battle for me, and I was mad that morning at the insults I'd been taking from those goddam Diaz officers in command there, General Navarro and that colonel of artillery of his, Tamborel. I was so mad I got into the thick of it

myself. I was there in the street with the shot-up remnants
of a platoon and we charged the headquarters building
where that aristocratic Tamborel was holed up. Did you
know he called me a pig when I gave him a chance to
surrender?

"I wanted to shoot that *cabrón* of a Porfirista so bad I
could taste it. And just before I had the chance somebody
lobbed a grenade into the room where Tamborel was, and I
turned back. And when I did, I saw you and Sammie there
and knew one of you had thrown the grenade, and then the
flash and the concussion blew the whole room apart.
Christ! what a grenade that one was! And a homemade one
at that. In the dust and the smoke I never saw you again.
But I recognized you when you came up the trail."

"I am sorry, *mi general,* if that day I cheated you of your
revenge."

"Well, it could have been Sammie. *No importa.* It is of
no importance," Villa said. Then he grinned. "Even if you
cheated me of my revenge, I will see you get a chance at
yours."

"How, *mi general?*"

"I am going to teach this *machón* Quintero not to out-
grow his *calzones.* I will find him for you and bring him to
Parral myself."

"Yourself?"

"Of course! Do you think I would miss a *duelo* like
that?" Villa said. "You set the *duelo* up for Cinco de Mayo.
The fifth of May, the holiday that commemorates the time a
handful of brave Mexicans defeated the French of Max-
imilian. And I guarantee to have Quintero there to meet
you."

It was hot on the Mapimí Desert.

Mora, the captain of the Dorados, the one who had led
Matt and Juanita to Villa's cave, said, "You think he will
come willingly, *mi general?*"

Villa wiped the sweat from his chubby face. "If I thought that, I would have sent you to bring him in," he said irritably. "*Eeeayy!* I had forgotten the heat of this place."

"And if he protests?" Captain Mora said.

"We'll shoot the bastard," Villa said.

"But *mi general*, that would spoil the *faena* at Parral, no?"

"You are right. There would be no *duelo* then, would there? Well, I will deal with Quintero when we get to Mapimí."

"Not that I object to shooting him," Captain Mora said.

"I know your feelings," Villa said. "Do not let them spoil your judgment."

Behind them trailed a half-dozen others, all clad in the tan clothes of the Dorados, all with revolvers on their hips.

"Eight of us," Mora said. "Quintero will have more than that at his ranch."

"Not Dorados."

Mora smiled. "You are right, *mi general*."

Quintero's hacienda was twenty kilometers south of Mapimí. Villa and Mora and the Dorados slept at Mapimí and rode out while the morning was still dark. They came into sight of the ranch buildings just as dawn was breaking.

There were a dozen guards lounging around the sprawling ranch house.

"Our Captain Quintero lives well, it appears," Mora said.

"Too well," Villa said. "Who in the hell does he think he is?"

Two of the guards called out to them. "*Alto!* Who goes?"

"Pancho Villa!

"*Sí, mi general,* now I recognize you," one of them said. He stood uncertainly, still holding a rifle raised, as if he was not sure what to do.

"Well?" Villa said.

The guard lowered the weapon. "I will tell Captain Quintero that you are here, *mi general*."

"Never mind. I will tell him myself," Villa said and rode on past the guards.

One of the guards said, "What can we do—when it's Villa?"

Quintero heard the voices outside his bedroom and jumped out of bed and rushed to a window. He began to swear. He hated trouble first thing in the morning. But he had been with Villa for three years now and had been in favor with the general because of his courage under fire. He trusted he could talk his way out of any trouble.

He pulled on his pants and hurried from the bedroom to the main part of the house. He was just in time to open the front door to the rap of Villa's gun butt.

"*Mi general!*" Quintero said. "It pleases me to see you! Pardon my appearance, but I, of course, did not know you were coming."

Villa shoved past him into the luxuriously furnished living room. "I am not concerned with how you look," he said. "I am concerned with what you have been doing."

"Doing, *mi general?* Why, awaiting your orders, *mi general*. Taking care of the affairs of my rancho while I await your orders." Quintero smiled easily.

Villa did not return the smile. He looked around the room and said to Mora, who had followed him in, "High living for a mere captain of horse soldiers, eh, Mora?"

"He lives well on a captain's pay," Mora said. "I would like to learn his secret."

"Well," Villa said, "maybe he will tell us." His eyes were on Quintero. "Tell me, *mi capitán*. How do you manage?"

"Manage, *mi general?* Well, I run a profitable ranch here."

"It appears so. It appears much more profitable than the other time I was here. Are you selling beef to the *federales?*"

"To the *federales?* You joke, *mi general.*"

"It is no joke, hombre. You have money coming from somewhere."

"*Mi general,* may I offer you breakfast? Let me call my *cocinera* to the kitchen."

"First you answer my questions," Villa said. "And do not give me any bullshit about making big money from cattle—unless you are selling beef to the Carrancistas."

"I swear not," Quintero said. "I swear I would never think of a thing like that. I do not know where you could hear a thing like that."

"Well," Villa said, "I didn't hear a thing like that. What I heard was that while I have been laid up you have been taking over this part of the state of Durango. Extorting money from banks and businessmen and even poor *peónes.* Using your reputation as one of my officers as a club and a threat. What do you say about all those rumors, *mi capitán?*"

"They are lies, *mi general.*"

"You know my orders are to leave the people alone. Only I decide when and where to take money—and then only for the Revolution. I do not take for myself. When I take, it is to pay my troops and buy weapons."

Quintero did not cringe, and Captain of the Dorados Mora had to credit him for that. The man had guts, all right, Mora thought.

Quintero stood straight and tall, and when he did he was looking down on the shorter Villa. He looked straight into Villa's upward stare. "*Mi general,*" he said, "I know your orders and always I have obeyed them. Have I ever shown a lack of courage in following your orders?"

He's changing the subject, Mora thought. This *hideputa*

knows how to get around the general. He knows the value the general puts on bravery.

"I do not question your courage," Villa said. "I question your honesty."

"I swear, *mi general*, that I have done nothing wrong."

"There is another matter," Villa said. "There is a gringo who claims you murdered his wife during the raid on Gunlock."

"So the gringo sergeant is still around."

"He is not a gringo sergeant anymore. He has deserted his army to search for you."

"He has some courage."

"He fought for me at the first Juárez."

Quintero nodded. Then he said, "The thing about his wife was unfortunate. An accident, really. I tried once to explain that to him. Before I tried to kill him."

"You have another chance. He challenges you to a gunfight in Parral."

"Well, I said he has courage."

"You will accept the challenge."

"You ask, *mi general?* Or you order?"

"Either way," Villa said, "what is your answer?"

"I accept, of course," Quintero said. "And *mi general*, I hope this will prove to you that I always follow your orders."

Villa gave him a long, scowling look, but Quintero did not fidget. "Well," Villa said finally, "call out your *cocinera*. I am ready for breakfast."

CHAPTER 11

MATT and the girl wound their way back through the rocky, barren peaks and ridges. At the end of the first day they camped in a stand of Jeffrey pine and recognized that they were now a half day's ride from the Durango-Parral road. Matt began to think about the gunfight.

"Do you believe, *chica*, that Villa will bring him? On Cinco de Mayo?"

"He is a man of his word, Mateo. You know it. He will go to Mapimí, get him, and bring him to Parral."

"On the fifth of May."

"*Sí*. On the fifth of May."

"This is a bad trail, *chica*. Is not the other route to Mapimí easier?"

"It is easier. It is the main route. But it comes south from Chihuahua City and enters Mapimí from the north. But still, there is the cursed desert to cross from that way too."

"I will be glad when we are back on the Parral road."

"By noon tomorrow, Mateo," she said.

In the morning they made good time because the trail was less rocky, although there was chaparral and manzanita, which hid the extent of their progress from them. But Matt knew they were making good time. He knew because he was leading a good pace and stopping only when Juanita argued for it. He was anxious now to get back to Parral, to start getting ready for that day in May. It was only two weeks away. He'd have to contact the impresario of the bullring. The girl and Gómez could help him with that. They would have to convince the impresario that it would be worth his while to stage a *mano a mano*—without bulls. Matt smiled grimly. He could almost see the impresario's face when they presented the idea.

His mind was on these things when he heard Juanita call out to him.

"*Qué pasa?*" he said.

"I heard horses up ahead."

He reined in his mount, halting the pack mule, and Juanita did likewise. They sat listening.

They heard nothing.

"What did you hear?" he said.

"I told you—I heard horses."

"So? There are horses? *Qué importa?* What does it matter? Let's go." He started on again, pushing along, with heavy growth on either side of the trail. They broke into a clearing.

The Indians were there waiting for them. They had army carbines raised.

Indians, for chrissakes! he thought. Indians wearing U.S. cavalry uniforms. And sitting cavalry saddles.

The Indian in the lead said, "Be smart!"

Matt looked at the six of them, all holding carbines at the ready. "I'm smart," he said.

"Good." The voice came from the side of the clearing. A gringo in charro garb moved out. He was sitting a Mexican stock saddle. He had a gun on his hip but nothing in his hand. He said, "You're Dunn."

Matt nodded.

"Name of Lacy. Scouting for Major Holcomb now. Had a brush with you in the Cobán *malpais,* few weeks back." Lacy studied what Matt was wearing. "Too dark then to tell you was the one that stole my clothes."

Matt swiftly recalled that night. He said, "Lieutenant Darwin—how bad?"

Lacy said, "Not bad. Your bullet plowed his arm."

"It was an accident."

"Figured so. Darwin did, too. But the major didn't."

"You're taking me in?"

Lacy nodded. "Sorry, Dunn. But Holcomb is making this well worth my while. He's one of the few independently wealthy career officers in the U.S. Army, the way I hear it. Family fortune. It must be so, because he's shelling out five hundred dollars to me from his pocket."

Matt stared at him, not speaking, until Lacy's eyes fell. Then he said, "Easy money for you."

Lacy met his eyes again and said, "Not as easy for me as you think. But it's more money than I ever had in one stake."

"And these Indians?"

"Apache scouts. Army brought twenty of them down from out of the reservation police at San Carlos. What for, I don't know. Ain't none of them ever been outside Arizona in their life. Hell, they don't know where the hell they are down here in Mexico. But they did follow your tracks from Parral after I found out the direction you took."

Matt turned and studied the Apaches one by one. There was no way he could read what they were thinking.

Lacy said, "Don't try anything rash, Dunn. These Injuns got orders to shoot if they have to. Not mine, the major's."

"Mean-looking bastards," Matt said in a low voice.

One of them, wearing three chevrons on his uniform sleeve, overheard him. He grinned at Matt, but with his teeth only. "Plenty mean," he said. "Don't forget it."

Lacy said to Matt, "That one's called Sergeant Rooster. And take his advice, Dunn. I been riding with them for some time now, and the one thing they got on their mind is to take a Mexican scalp. But if they can't get a Mexican, I reckon they'd lift one off a gringo. You got to figure their life is pretty tame nowadays, and they ain't got much to brag about. They lift your hair and they'll be big men back on the reservation."

"It's nice to have ambition," Matt said. "Sergeant Rooster is a funny name for an Apache, though."

"A lot of them got crazy names they use, them that don't have Spanish ones," Lacy said. "Not many whites can pronounce a real Apache name, so they all been given nicknames. Like Loco Jim and Hell Yet Suey and Skitty Joe. I hear Rooster got his from killing his cousin in an argument over a cockfight."

Sergeant Rooster shook his head. "Big lie," he said. "No kill cousin. Kill brother." He grinned again at Matt.

"He's got a nice smile, anyway," Matt said.

"All right, Dunn, give us your weapons," Lacy said. "It's a long ride back to Bachíniva and the major."

Long ride is right, Matt thought, as they followed the twisting trail under the eyes of the six Apache scouts. The Apaches may have been lost down here in Mexico, but they sure knew how to watch a prisoner. Lacy had ordered the captives' ankles lashed under their horses' bellies, but the unreadable hardness of the Apaches' eyes bound Matt more strongly than the bonds. He had the feeling they were childishly eager to kill him. What they would like to do to Juanita, he could only guess.

Lacy rode up front, with Matt a few feet on his right, Juanita on his left, and the Apaches strung along behind them. The trail widened as they got closer to the Durango road.

Lacy seemed bothered by what he was doing. Once Matt turned his head and caught the scout looking at him.

Lacy said, "Those duds you're wearing. I reckon you needed them bad or you wouldn't have stole them off of me."

"Stealing's not a habit with me," Matt said.

"I was mad at the time," Lacy said. He hesitated, then

went on: "But even that don't take the sting out of what I'm doing."

"Five hundred bucks can buy a lot of clothes," Matt said.

"Yeah."

They rode in silence for a while. Then Lacy said, "Goddamit, Matt, I know what happened to you back there in Gunlock."

"So does the major," Matt said.

Lacy scowled. "I ain't the goddam major! I'd be better off if I was." He relapsed into a brooding silence and rode staring straight ahead.

A couple of hours later they halted for a relief break. "Road is just ahead," Lacy said. He untied the ropes from their ankles. Juanita moved off into the brush. When she returned, they remounted.

Sergeant Rooster rode up and pointed at the captives' feet.

Lacy shook his head. "Leave the ties off," he said.

The Apache stared at him for a moment, then nodded and grinned and dropped back with the rest.

"Didn't seem to make him mad," Matt said.

"He's hoping you make a break for it," Lacy said.

"Who said we ever whipped the Apaches?"

"It took a long time to think we did."

"Yeah," Matt said.

After a while Lacy said, "You think you could take that bastard Quintero if you met up with him? Darwin told me his name."

"Him or me, I got to try."

"Knowing what he done to your wife, I'd like to see you get your chance."

"Well?"

Lacy didn't answer for a while. Then he said, "No. Not five hundred dollars' worth."

"Can't fault you for that," Matt said. "A man's got to think of his future."

"That bothers me some, too," Lacy said. He spurred his horse up ahead and rode alone.

Juanita rode close beside Matt and said in a low voice, "That major, Mateo—he will never let you go, is it not so?"

"It is so."

"Then you must try to escape."

"You have a plan?"

"Perhaps."

He looked back at the Apaches, who were trailing a hundred feet behind, and then at Lacy riding by himself up in front. "What is your plan?"

"The Apaches, they would shoot you, no?"

"Lacy says so—and I believe it."

"Would they shoot me?"

He turned his head and studied her. "Do not even consider it," he said. "They have nothing against killing women."

"But if I tried to escape and they came after me, it would give you a chance."

"I said not to consider it."

"I would take the risk, Mateo."

"No!" he said. "And I do not want to hear more of that."

She was quiet for a while, then she said, "The cowboy, he is not a bad man, true? Not like the Apaches."

"True. He is only doing a job for money."

"The cowboy is the key, then."

"How?"

"I do not know, not yet. But we must think of something."

She is right, Matt thought. Once Holcomb gets me, I'm through. He'll bring me to a court-martial. What we heard in Cobán was that he wanted me for desertion. Then I shot Darwin, and he'll charge that that was intentional. Hell, it will be a general court, if he has his way with the top brass. I could get a life sentence.

And I'd never get a chance at Quintero.

"Think, Mateo," Juanita said softly. "Think very hard."

"Yeah," he said.

Presently he rode up to Lacy's side. He said, "There's the matter of the girl. She's a Mexican citizen. The major has no authority over her."

Lacy nodded. "I've been thinking on that, too."

"Did Holcomb order you to bring her in?"

"Don't recall he mentioned her."

"Well, then."

"Well, what?"

"Let her go, Lacy. What harm can she do?"

Lacy looked at him for a long, studying moment. Then he laughed, long and loud. "Look, Dunn. I been working in Mexico for near a dozen years. I'd know what that girl is, even if I hadn't learned her background from the people up in Cobán. She's a *soldadera* — leastwise she used to be. What harm could she do?! Man, she's as dangerous as a black widow spider."

"Don't know what law you can hold her on," Matt said.

"Law? I'll tell you what law—the law of survival. We've got a lot of miles before we reach Bachíniva. If I turned her loose, she'd get a gun somewhere, you can bet on it." Then, as if to himself, he said, "And I ain't about to get myself bushwhacked by a Mexican pepper pot. Hell, that girl is in love with you."

"Do you think she'd take on single-handed you and those six Apaches back there?"

"Hell, she'd take on the whole U.S. cavalry if they had you in custody."

"It doesn't seem right she should be hauled in on account of me."

"I ain't concerned just now with right," Lacy said. "I'm concerned with safe. We get to Bachíniva, the major can decide what to do with her. Don't argue no more about it."

Matt dropped back to ride again beside Juanita.

"Anything?" she said.

"There is one way, maybe," Matt said. He looked back at the Apaches again. When he spoke his voice was lowered, and she listened intently to hear him. He finished and she nodded soberly.

"I will be ready," she said.

"It will be at that place where the pass narrows. That last pass before the trail reaches the Durango road."

"I remember the place."

"We have to get the cowboy back here with us. That, or we will have to catch up with him."

But, as if in answer to their need, Lacy reined up and waited for them to rejoin him. The Apaches still held their distance behind them.

Matt said to the girl, "I'll stay on his right side, the side on which he wears his pistol. You stay on the right of me."

"He has a carbine in his saddle scabbard," she said. "Do not forget that, Mateo."

"I am gambling he will not use it," Matt said. "Or that he will not have time."

"I pray it is so."

As they reached him Lacy said, "It's time we rode together. I got no hard feelings against you."

"Me neither," Matt said, and he reached out fast with his left hand and jerked Lacy's six-gun from its holster.

Lacy grabbed for it with his right hand and missed. "You damned fool!" he said.

An army .45 automatic barked from back by the Apaches, and the slug kicked up dirt between their horses.

Lacy pivoted left away from Matt, swearing at Matt or the Apaches or both. The next shot went by Matt's ear so close he felt the wind whip of it. He'd heard old cavalry stories about the Indians' poor marksmanship with a handgun, and he hoped there was some truth in them.

"Ride!" he shouted to Juanita, and together they raced

into the defile of the pass, here strewn with huge, fallen boulders.

He heard the crack of a Springfield and heard the scary whine of a bullet ricochet off a rock behind them.

"Go!" he said to the girl and twisted in his saddle and saw the ugly face of Sergeant Rooster appear above a boulder. He flung a wild shot in Rooster's direction and the Apache dropped from sight.

The Apache did not reappear in the defile, and Matt turned and kicked heels to the sorrel and it stretched out and caught up with Juanita's mount.

There was wild exhilaration in her face as she turned to look at him. "*Vámonos*, Mateo — we are free!" And she raced her horse in pure exuberance.

The sorrel matched her pace easily as they reached the Durango road and turned north toward Parral. They continued to run until they topped a rise and started a long descent that extended to the base of another rise in the distance.

"Slow down, *chica*," Matt called then. "It will not do to kill the horses."

She slowed. "You are right, Mateo. It is a long way to Parral." Then she said, "That Apache *feo*—the ugliest one —did you kill him?"

"I did not try," he said.

She gave him a puzzled look. "*Por qué no?*"

He shook his head. "He is part of the cavalry now. I cannot kill one of my own army."

She shrugged and looked straight ahead. "You gringos are all crazy," she said.

They had enough of a lead so that they reached the next rise before the Apaches topped the one behind. As they descended he spied another rise in the distance. He remembered this stretch as a long series of ups and downs. If they could maintain their lead they might keep out of rifle range of Lacy and the Apaches. But what happens, he wondered, when the road flattens out, as he knew it did before they reached the town of Ocampo?

Juanita must have been having like thoughts, because the exuberance was gone from her face. She said, "They will keep tracking us forever, Mateo. The Apaches will sight us when the road gets flat."

"How far to Ocampo?" he said.

"Perhaps twenty kilometers."

"Twelve miles," he said. "Do you have any friends there who might help us?"

"I have a cousin," she said. "But I have forgotten his name."

"One cousin, though, could not do much."

They rode in silence for several minutes, then she said, "A thing has come to me, Mateo. Did you see the monument in the plaza when we came through before?"

"In Ocampo? I took no notice."

"It is a great rock, on the side of which there is a plaque of beaten copper."

"What about this monument?" he said.

"Many years ago, perhaps thirty or more, a raiding band of Geronimo's Apaches came out of the Sierra Madre and killed most of the men and women of Ocampo."

"And this plaque?"

"Engraved there are the names of all those killed. All Mexicans hate Apaches, but the people of places like Ocampo, and of Bavispe in Sonora, they hate the Apaches worst of all. They have never forgotten what the Apaches did to their families."

"You are sure of this?"

"Yes."

"That may help us," Matt said.

"If we can reach Ocampo," Juanita reminded him. "Only half the distance there is hilly *cuestas* like this."

"That leaves five or six miles of open road."

"Can we outrun them, Mateo?"

"I don't know." He knew the sorrel could, but he did not know about Juanita's horse.

"The *alazán* can do it," she said. "And it is you they will be after."

"What good would it be? What could I do alone in Ocampo? Do I have a cousin there? Maybe they do not like gringos there, either."

"They like them better than Apaches," she said.

Stubbornly, he replied, "If we reach Ocampo, it will be together."

Dust kicked up ahead of them in the road, and a moment later he heard the crack of a Springfield. He looked back and saw an Apache lying prone on top of the last rise, the sun glinting off his rifle barrel.

They were only halfway up the slope to the next rise, and Matt swore under his breath. While he had been talking at least one of the Apaches had run his horse and got within shooting range of them.

He spurred his mount and Juanita's matched his pace. Behind them the Springfield kept popping.

The brow of the rise seemed to get no closer. I hope they're lousy shots, Matt thought. Then they topped the rise and, for a while, had cover.

"Keep them running," Matt called. But after a short time he pulled the sorrel in. They couldn't afford to expend the mounts. There was that five- or six-mile stretch up there waiting for them.

They rode steadily for an hour or more and judged that they must have kept their distance, because no more rifle shots came from the Apaches. Matt wondered if Lacy had joined in on the fusillade back there. It seemed that Lacy had little control over the Apaches, especially if they decided to go scalp hunting, now that they had an excuse.

It didn't seem likely that Holcomb would have wanted him killed. He'd probably become carried away when he'd given the order to bring Matt in. Matt imagined it would be kind of hard to explain the finer points to an Apache.

"Mateo!"

"*Sí.*"

"We have passed the last *cuesta.*"

Ahead of them stretched the five miles of open road ending in the town of Ocampo. True, there was rock- and brush-covered terrain on either side that might afford them cover. But once in that *matorral,* they'd be no match for six Apaches. That kind of terrain was the Apaches' native ground.

They'd have to run for it. "Now!" he said and took off fast.

At a half mile he looked back and the bunch of them were topping the last rise. They saw Matt's and the girl's horses running, whooped, and came on fast themselves, yelping like coyotes chasing a rabbit. Lacy was behind them, trying to catch up. It all settled down to a horse race.

He appreciated the sorrel, and Juanita's roan too. Her horse had more bottom than he would have expected; it just wouldn't let the sorrel pull away. He wondered how long it could keep up.

During the last mile a few wild pistol shots blasted the air. Then they burst into the town and into the plaza with the big rock that Juanita had mentioned.

A scattering of townspeople had heard the shooting and rushed to see the finish of the race from the plaza. There was a cantina facing the plaza, with several horses tied at its hitch rail. A dozen charros spilled out through the door to see the excitement.

Matt caught all this with a glance as he slid the sorrel to a halt. He yelled to the people, "Those are Apaches chasing! Can you help us?"

And Juanita called, "I am the cousin of Vásquez!"

A charro running in the lead, a short, stocky man who looked part drunk and wore his six-gun in a high-hung holster on his hip, Mexican style, hollered, "I know Vásquez! Apaches, you say?"

"Apaches!" Juanita answered.

The stocky charro jerked out his gun.

The Apaches, with Lacy trailing, tore into the fringe of the town yelling war cries.

The charro fired his gun, the horse of an Apache went down, and the rider sailed over its head and came down running.

Another charro reached the first one's side and he fired too. Within seconds most of the charros were blasting away. The Apaches reined up hard, pivoted, and started away. The one on foot was caught by the last rider and scrambled up behind his saddle. They pulled back out of range of the charro *pistoleros*.

"*Gracias, amigos!*" Matt said.

"*Por nada*," the stocky charro said. "Against Apaches, we take anybody's part. The monument here will tell you why. And for the cousin of Vásquez, especially." He seemed to sober slightly as a thought struck him. "But from this distance, cousin of Vásquez," he said to Juanita, "it appears the Apaches wear the clothes of the gringo *caballería*. Stolen, perhaps?"

Matt said, "Thieving *cabrónes*, aren't they?"

The charro focused his eyes unsteadily on Matt. "By your accent you are gringo. We do not like gringos here, either."

"This one is my friend," Juanita said.

"That makes a difference."

Matt looked down the roadway and he could see the Apaches having a discussion with Lacy. Almost immediately Lacy broke away from the bunch and rode slowly toward the plaza, holding his hand up as if making the Indian sign for peace.

"The damn fool!" Matt said to Juanita. "They will mistake him for an Apache." He said to the charros, "Do not shoot! He is a gringo vaquero."

"Why does he wear Mexican clothes?"

"Somebody stole his own," Matt said. He yelled now at Lacy, "Get your damn hand down!"

Lacy dropped his hand and shouted back. "Let me come in, Matt. Don't shoot. Let's talk about this."

"Come ahead."

Lacy rode into the plaza and flicked his eyes over the peons and over the armed charros. His carbine was still in its scabbard. He said in English, "Looks like you found help. Friends of yours?"

"They just hate Apaches," Matt said, looking aside at the charros as he gestured with his head. One of them had brought a bottle from the cantina and they were passing it around, at the same time keeping their eyes on Lacy.

"What does he say, this other gringo?" the stocky charro said. He had just taken a long swig from the bottle and wiped his mouth on his left sleeve. "Is it your wish I put a bullet into him?"

"Please, no!" Matt said. "He is an amigo."

"*Some amigo!* He rides with Apaches." The charro turned to Juanita: "What say you, pretty cousin of Vásquez?"

"The Apaches are the enemy, not this one," Juanita said. She said it reluctantly, as if she said it only because she knew Matt wanted it that way.

The bottle was going around and some of the charros from the cantina were getting impatient.

One of them said to the stocky one, "I do not like the sight of those murdering Apache *cabrónes* sitting out there as if they had the right. What do you say, Pablo? Shall we mount up and go make *good* Apaches out of them? We are two to their one."

"Even a dead Apache is not a good Apache," Pablo said. "However, he is much better than a live one."

"*Vámonos,* then!" the other said and started to cross the plaza to where the horses were tied in front of the cantina.

At that moment Sergent Rooster took it in his head to suddenly spur hell-bent for the plaza. The other Apaches followed, with their .45 automatics blasting at anything and everything, and filling the air with war cries.

Lacy said, "The crazy bastards are trying to count coup."

The Mexicans tried to get behind the monument rock, all except the half-drunk charros, who stood in the open and returned the Apache fire. The Apaches wheeled and raced away, still yelling.

Short, chunky Pablo, the charro who had first come to their aid, was lying on his back just beneath the copper plaque that commemorated those killed by Geronimo's Apaches. Blood spurted out of a wound in his chest.

Down the road, the Apaches disappeared into the *matorral.*

The other charros hostered their weapons and looked at Pablo. Matt could feel they were turning mean. The Apaches were gone from sight, but the gringo who had ridden with them was sitting his horse right there in front of them. Matt could see a dozen pairs of bloodshot black eyes sizing Lacy up. He said, "Watch it, Lacy. That liquor is causing some fuzzy thinking."

A charro said bluntly, nodding toward the cowboy. "That gringo is one of them."

"I tell you no," Matt said.

"You gringo *cabrónes!* You got Pablo killed."

Juanita said in panic. "Not Mateo!" She reached out and grabbed his arm. "He is my friend!"

"Him, yes," the charro said. "But this other, he is not. I

saw him chasing you along with the Apaches. We will take his life in exchange for Pablo's."

Matt pulled out the gun he had taken from Lacy. "Do not try it, amigo!" he said. "I am sorry this happened. You helped us, and I am sorry about Pablo."

There was a long moment while the charros stared. The hostility grew in their eyes. The one who had spoken before finally said, "You gringo loco! I will tell you how it must be. We will not kill this other gringo who rode with the Apaches who killed our *compadre*, Pablo."

"Good!" Matt said.

"No," the charro went on, "we will not kill him." He paused. "You will. With that pistol you hold in your hand. You will kill him or we will let the Apaches ride in and take you."

Juanita watched Matt's face.

Matt was sweating now. He said, "I cannot do that, amigo."

The charro said, "He is a peculiar friend. He rides with Apaches who chase you."

"He was given that job by the gringo army," Matt said. "It is just that he cannot control the Apaches. I will tell you now, the Apaches are police for the gringo army."

The charro was drunk enough that he only half listened. "You talk much," he said. "Will you kill this gringo bastard or will we let the Apaches in?"

Juanita still kept her eyes on Matt.

Matt was silent.

"So," the charro said. "You are on your own." He gestured to the others, and they picked up the body of Pablo and moved toward the cantina, leaving Matt and Lacy and Juanita alone.

They all three stared up the road to where the Apaches had disappeared.

"Well?" Lacy said.

"I don't know what the hell to do with you now," Matt said.

"Yeah. Well, I owe you for what you just done."

"Does that help?"

"It's like you said, I can't control those bastards."

"Will you help us stand them off?"

Lacy did not speak at once. Then he said, "They'll get you anyway, Matt. You know that, don't you?"

"Maybe."

"You'll never get away from them now. And I'm on army payroll. I can't fire on the military scouts."

"You're on Holcomb's payroll on this," Matt said. "His personal money. You told me that yourself."

"That, too," Lacy said. Then: "You got to understand this. I been punching cattle down here and other places since I was fifteen. All those years of pounding my butt against a stock saddle. That ain't as bad as pounding one of them split McClellans, maybe, but a cowboy rides a hell of a lot more hours a year than a cavalryman does. I'm tired of taking crap from ranch owners and Mex *hacendados*. I'm getting too old for this business, older than my age. I always wanted to get me a little place up Arizona way. Just run a few head, maybe, and take it easy. But I never could get me a stake. Now I got the chance, the one chance I'll likely ever get. Five hundred bucks. That'll get me a homestead, one-sixty acres near some government graze. I got to go through with this. I may never get another chance."

"I ought to put a bullet through your mercenary heart," Matt said angrily.

Lacy nodded. "Go ahead," he said. "If you think you can do it."

Matt swore.

Juanita, eyes flashing, spoke up for the first time. "If you do not have the heart to kill him, Mateo, give me the gun and I will do it for you."

He shook his head. "Dammit! he's army now. One of the 12th. It'd be like killing one of my own outfit."

"Then for the love of God, tie him up, hands and feet, and leave him here. We must go."

Matt glanced toward the cantina door. "The charros . . ."

"So what they do to him is not our business," she said.

"It is better that I tie him and we take him with us," Matt said.

"Why?"

He searched for an excuse. "Because if the Apaches ride in, they will free him."

"All right, then. But let us steal fresh horses." She gestured to those of the charros tied up in front of the cantina.

Again he shook his head.

"You are too good to steal?"

"Not that. But do you think those charros aren't watching? One move toward their horses and we're all dead."

She sighed. "So be it, Mateo. Tie the hands of this one and let us hope we can reach Parral ahead of the Apaches. There is no hope trying to take another route. They are too good as trackers."

In a few moments they were on their way down the road toward Parral. Matt said, "Let's go!" But the horses and the mule had run too much. Even the sorrel would do no more than a trot. The other two would only walk. Matt dropped back to keep pace. There was one consolation, he thought: the mounts of the Apaches could not do any better.

But what would happen now? You couldn't figure on a bunch of drunken charros to side with you in every town. If they reached Parral, there was Gómez, but what could he do? Rouse the people of Parral to protect them, maybe. At the moment that looked like their only chance. It now settled down to a chase between exhausted mounts. If they could maintain a distance out of range of their pursuers, they might make it.

They rode four miles, and there was no sight of the

Apaches behind them. The brush here was dense on either side of the road.

Lacy, riding with his hands lashed, saw Matt's backward glance and said, "Maybe they gave up. You never can tell about an Injun."

There was something in his tone that bothered Matt. Lacy's words were said too easily. I can never trust the bastard, Matt thought. Not when he has his mind set on getting a grubstake. In a lot of ways he's a good enough man, I guess, but he's got a dollar sign in each eye.

He was still thinking about this when a voice sounded in the heavy brush alongside them. "Hey, Sergeant! Put up your hands!"

Matt could not tell just where the voice came from. He drew the gun he had taken from Lacy and pointed it at the cowboy. He called, "Show yourself or I'll put a bullet into him."

There was a laugh. "Go ahead. One less white-eyes." A gun fired and Matt almost jumped from his saddle. "I don't fool no more. Throw gun down, put hands up. Or I shoot girl."

Matt hesitated.

"I don't tell again."

Matt dropped the weapon.

Sergeant Rooster stepped out into the roadway, grinning. "You think I miss this close, Sergeant? I only shoot signal. Others bring up horses now. Me, I leave horse and run long way through scrub on foot. Like all Apache, I fast runner. Go fifty mile in one day easy." He laughed again. "Run like *rooster*, hey? And Major Holcomb, I think he like much what I do."

Twenty minutes later the other Apaches appeared on the road, leading five horses. Sergeant Rooster wave his arm at them and they mounted and rode up to join him.

"All right, Sergeant," Rooster said. "You got one horse

killed. So Apache ride yours. You walk. Walk all the way to Bachíniva."

"I'll buy a horse in Parral," Lacy said.

Sergeant Rooster shrugged. "All right. You lucky, Sergeant. You only have to walk to Parral."

Matt, walking, said to Juanita, who was riding sullenly beside him, "Too bad your cousin did not show at the plaza. Things might have gone better for us."

She said, "They would have gone well anyway, if you were not such a fool. You should have let the charros kill the cowboy." She rode in silence, then said, "Anyway, I do not really have a cousin there."

Matt said, surprised, "But they knew him. When you gave the name of Vásquez—"

She made a scoffing sound. "In any Mexican town," she said, "there is always a Vásquez."

CHAPTER 12

IN the few weeks since Matt and the girl had passed through Bachíniva, the place had changed. Now it was the location of the southernmost detachment of the expedition forces, and this gave the drowsy town a slight bustle that hadn't been there before.

Holcomb's troops were tented a mile out of the cluster of adobes, far enough to make the major's off-limits ruling on the town enforceable yet near enough to make it convenient to purchase supplies and obtain water from the town well.

Lacy and the Apache scout escort took their captives directly to the major's headquarters tent. Several troopers eyed them curiously, and some called cautious greetings to Matt. They all knew the story behind Matt's desertion and most sympathized with him, though few cared to have the major know of their sympathy.

Lacy spoke to the major's orderly, who stepped inside the tent. In a moment he reappeared and nodded for Lacy to enter.

Holcomb said, "Well?"

"We've got them, Major."

"Them?"

"I brought back the girl too."

"Good. Any trouble?"

Lacy hesitated. He hated to make things worse for Matt,

but he knew the Apaches would talk, if only to boast of their recapture of the prisoners after the escape attempt. Whoever said Indians were closemouthed hadn't known any, he thought. Better that he be frank with the major, since the word would be out soon enough. "They tried to get away," Lacy said. "Nothing serious."

"Another charge added," Holcomb said. "Resisting arrest and attempting to escape custody." He went over to a footlocker in a corner of the tent and took from it a roll of greenbacks. He counted off ten fifty-dollar bills and handed them to Lacy.

Lacy shoved the wad into his pocket without counting it. He said, "By rights, you ought to pay me with fifty pieces of silver."

"You've listened too much to Lieutenant Darwin," Holcomb said. "The girl, is she the same one that helped him at Cobán?"

Lacy nodded.

"I've got a place for her too," Holcomb said. "Tell the orderly to send the prisoners in."

Lacy held the flap as Matt and Juanita entered. Without thought, Matt saluted.

Holcomb's face reddened. He said angrily, "Don't you know you don't rate a salute?"

Matt dropped his arm.

"Answer me, goddamit!"

"Yes, sir."

"Yes, sir, *what?*"

"Yes, sir, I don't rate a salute, I guess."

"You *guess!*"

"Yes, sir."

Holcomb fought down his anger. Then he said, "Let me read off the charges against you. First, desertion. And that during the pursuit of an enemy. Second, assaulting and wounding a commissioned officer—your own Lieutenant

Darwin. And now, according to Lacy here, escape from custody and resisting re-arrest by authorized military police."

Matt was silent.

"Well?"

Matt said slowly, "During the raid, Quintero, one of the Villista officers, raped and killed my wife, sir. . . ." He let the words hang, the horror of what happened there at Gunlock striking him mute.

"That is no excuse, soldier."

". . . She died in my arms from burns he caused her. . . . She begged me to find him and kill him."

For a moment Holcomb appeared impressed. Then his old belligerence returned and he said, "Granted that the original circumstances were extenuating, you have still continuously compounded the violations of army regulations and the Articles of War. I have no alternative but to hold you for a general court-martial when one can be convened."

". . . And I could maybe kill him if I only had until the fifth of May," Matt continued, as if he had not been listening to Holcomb.

"What?" Holcomb said sharply.

Lacy said, "The fifth of May, Major. Cinco de Mayo. A big Mexican holiday. And Dunn, here, is scheduled to meet the Villista that murdered his wife in a gunfight in Parral on that date. In the bullring there."

"*What?*"

"I'm telling you what he told me, Major," Lacy said. "The girl will tell you the same thing. When me and the Apaches took him, they had just been to see Villa himself down in Durango, and he agreed to arrange it."

Holcomb's face was red again. "What kind of a cock-and-bull story are you giving me?"

The cowboy-scout shrugged. "I'm just passing on to you

what he told me." He paused. "And Major, I believe him."

"Then you're a damn fool." The major suddenly pressed his hand against his ribs where the wound he had received at Corrales was healing. All this talk was making it pain him again. There was another pain that wasn't healing nearly as well. The pain of knowing that Pershing was highly displeased with his handling of the confrontation there against Colonel Brito of the *federales*. He forced himself to adopt a calmer tone and said, "Dunn, this thing about a gunfight in a bullring—that's a damn lie, isn't it?"

"No, sir."

"Well then, dammit," Holcomb said, "give me the details."

Matt looked at him blankly. He seemed to have trouble recovering from the terrible memory of Molly in the shack at Gunlock.

"Dunn!"

Matt stayed silent another long moment. Then he said in a monotone, "When I couldn't find Quintero—the one who killed Molly—I got the idea to meet him in a duel. Villa is fixing it for him to meet me in Parral on Cinco de Mayo."

"In a bullfight arena?"

"Yes, sir."

"You think this Mexican will accept your challenge?"

"I think so. Villa gave me his word he'd be there."

The major seized on this. "Villa. Will Villa be there, too?"

Matt shrugged. "He'd maybe want to see it."

Lacy's eyes were on Holcomb now. The sonofabitch! he thought. I think I know what he's thinking.

Holcomb broke off his questioning abruptly. "We'll talk some more about this later," he said to Matt. "Meanwhile, I've already requisitioned the town jail for use as a temporary guardhouse. You'll be held there awaiting further action."

Matt said, "The girl, sir, she is a Mexican citizen."

Holcomb said, "Like I told Lacy, I've got a place for her too."

"In the guardhouse?"

"I wouldn't waste her talents there. No, I've been think-ing of a small edition of what Pershing has allowed to be set up near the base command at Colonia Dublán. A fenced-off compound for a brothel. With a medic to inspect the girls. It keeps the troops from slipping off to pick up V.D. from local chippies." Holcomb stared into Matt's eyes. "The girl could be the first recruit here. Is she clean, soldier?"

"Goddam you!" Matt said. "She isn't a whore."

"That's another charge against you," the major said. "Gross insubordination and verbal abuse of a commanding officer. Soldier, you could be looking at a life sentence, do you know that?"

Matt struggled with his voice, then said, "Sir, the girl has worked in cantinas, but she is not a *puta*."

For the first time, Juanita understood a word they were saying, and she knew it must refer to her. "*No soy puta!*" she screamed at Holcomb, "*pendejo mayor!*"

"What did she say?" Holcomb said to Lacy.

"I am not a whore, stupid major!" Lacy rolled the words on his tongue as if he enjoyed repeating them. Then his tone changed and he said, "I wouldn't try nothing like you were talking about, Major. This girl has been a *soldadera* in the Revolution. That means 'girl soldier,' and I mean a fighting one. Some trooper tries to make her lay and he'd have better luck making love to a wildcat."

To Matt, the bare adobe walls of the cell were suffocat-ing. The cell comprised the whole jail, eight feet square maybe, with a single small, high window with iron bars and a heavy wood door made from old railroad ties bolted together.

Sergeant Rooster and one of the other Apaches who'd escorted him there threw a pair of blankets onto the dirt floor and left him a slop bucket and a bucket of water with a dipper.

Sergeant Rooster grinned. "Try to get out," he said to Matt. "One Apache be on guard all the time. We like you to get out."

Some chance, Matt thought as Rooster slammed the door shut, bolted it, and fastened the bolt with a padlock and chain.

It was after dark when Matt heard them fussing with the lock. There was considerable fumbling and then the crude door was tugged open and Major Holcomb stood there, flanked by another of the Apaches and by Private Oursler, the major's orderly, who held a mess kit of food.

From long habit Matt got up from the spread blankets and stood at attention as the major entered.

Oursler stooped and placed the mess kit on the floor near the blankets, then stepped back. When Holcomb did not give the order "At ease," Matt dropped his stiff stance anyway.

The major got right to the point. "I want to hear from you again this thing about the challenge you sent to that raider."

"I told you how it is," Matt said. "Villa liked the idea for reasons of his own, and said he'd see that Quintero came to meet me. Even if Villa didn't order it, I figured Quintero would take up the challenge. He's what the Mexicans call *muy macho.*"

"I know all about their goddam *macho*," Holcomb muttered.

"Well, Quintero has got it in plenty. And he's proud of his reputation for using a gun. He'll be there, I'm sure of it."

"And you think Villa will be there?"

"There's a strong chance."

"Interesting," Holcomb said. "Too bad you got all these charges piled up against you, Dunn. Damned if I wouldn't like to let you and that sonofabitch walk each other down."

"Let me go meet him, Major. It's something I promised Molly I'd do. If I lose, you're saved the trouble of getting me court-martialed. If I win, you got my word I'll give myself up when it's over."

Holcomb shook his head. "Even if I trusted you, which I don't, the charges are in the squadron records. No way I could turn you loose without jeopardizing myself." For a few seconds he stood there, seeming to waver in indecision, giving Matt a long, thoughtful look. Then abruptly he shrugged and turned away. Over his shoulder he said from the doorway, "I'll leave the lantern. It'll give you a light to eat by."

Then he was gone, Oursler and the Apache guard with him.

First decent thing the bastard ever did for me, Matt thought, leaving me the lantern.

He sat cross-legged on the blankets, leaned against the mud brick wall, and began to eat from the mess kit.

While he ate his eyes rested on the heavy timbered door. No way a man could break through it. Even if there wasn't a scalp-hungry Apache on the other side of it.

The lantern sputtered slightly and he reached quickly to turn up the wick, remembering suddenly that he had no matches to relight it if it went out.

That's when he looked again at the heavy wood door.

He listened hard for any sound of the Apache guard outside. There was none. Holcomb, he knew, was using the Apaches for this duty because the troopers of the squadron were sympathetic to Matt. The Apaches were not. Matt could vouch for that. But had Holcomb taken the guard away with him? Had he trusted that none of the locals of the town would dare bother the lock? After all, the major was detaining Juanita at the camp, and she was the only

Mexican who would try to free the incarcerated gringo.

His plan began to form while he finished the food. He took the dipper from the water bucket, wiped it dry on his shirt, and carefully balanced it across the top of the mess kit.

Then he took the lantern and shook it slightly near his ear and heard the sloshing of the kerosene in the reservoir. It sounded close to full.

He unscrewed the filler cap and began to tilt the lighted lantern to pour the kerosene from it into the dipper. As the lantern tilted, the wick sputtered, and he felt a quick fear that it might go out. He was concerned too, that the flame might ignite the kerosene as he poured and would set him on fire.

The thought of Molly in flames increased both his fear of the flame and his determination to escape. He poured until most of the fluid had gone from the lantern into the dipper, leaving just enough to supply the wick for a short time.

He replaced the filler cap, set the lamp down again on the floor, and picked up the bucket of water. He sloshed the contents carefully over one of the blankets until it was soaked through, then dragged it over to the high window and reached up and tied a corner of it to one of the iron bars. He spread the blanket over his body, testing it as a heat shield. It was cold and wet against his neck. Matt hoped it would do the job.

He came out from under the blanket and listened again for a guard. No sound.

He picked up the dipper of kerosene, moved close to the door, and tossed the liquid over the lower portion. Then he stepped back, took the lantern from the floor, and threw it. It smashed against the door and a sheet of flame shot up.

The searing scorch that struck his face surprised and terrified him. He had underestimated the heat generated by the blaze in the tight confines of his tiny cell. He fled to the wet blanket hanging from the window bar and dived under its protection. He thrust the top of the blanket as high as he could reach and sucked in great gasps of outside air that came through the opening. He felt a wave of panic and with anguish imagined how Molly must have suffered.

Matt heard the crackle of the burning timbers. He wanted to look, but he could not drag himself away from the air of the window.

Smoke now sought the window, too; it seeped around the edges of the blanket and was sucked into his lungs along with the air. He could feel the heat through the blanket; the wetness was going. It seemed the heat grew more intense, the smoke thicker, his coughing and gasping worse. He took a final breath of air and dug his way out of the draping blanket and into the engulfing smoke. He dropped to his hands and knees and crawled to where he saw the ember glow of the smoldering door. He peered at it, his held breath swelling the veins in his face. It was still intact.

A raging desperation took him, and he twisted and drew back his leg, kicked out hard with his boot sole, and felt the charred timber break through. He gathered himself up, dived headfirst at the opening, felt the hot edges claw at his shoulders, and landed hard on the cool earth beyond.

He lay there for several seconds, the wind knocked out of him, feeling as if he'd broken his breastbone and possibly one leg. Then he began to crawl away from the door and his hand touched a metallic something and he closed his fingers around the padlock that was supposed to lock the door. The bail of it was open.

He looked back at the door and, in the faint glow from the smoldering pieces he had broken loose, saw that the chain that was supposed to bind the timber bolt was hanging loose.

The door had been unlocked all the time! And where, he wondered, was the Apache guard? What the hell was going on?

He stood up and knew his leg wasn't broken but might be sprained. And for the first time he saw the dim figures standing in the shadows, silent and curious, all white peon clothes and straw hats. He understood. They had seen the flames of the *calabozo* and had come to investigate. But not too close. They were held back by fear of the gringo major.

And then Juanita came riding out of the darkness on her own horse and leading Matt's sorrel. She was breathing hard, but she said, "Mateo! Are you all right?"

"I think so."

"I saw the flames. But I was still far off—"

"How did you escape the camp?"

"The major let me go."

"The major!" It reminded Matt that he had better get away from there fast. He climbed on the sorrel and said, "Let's ride."

"Back to Parral," she said and led off at a gallop.

Only after they had put a mile behind them did he call to her to slow down. "How did you get the horses?"

"From the major. I think. When they turned me loose, they had the horses saddled and ready. And they told me to go."

Matt shook his head. "It does not make sense."

Juanita said, "I agree. The major must have known I would go first to aid you. He even told me you were in the *calabozo*."

All the hell and danger he had gone through to burn out the door—and all the time the thing was open. It sure made a man feel like a damn fool. He kicked the sorrel in the ribs in his irritation.

And the sonofabitch of a major had kept their pack mule.

It was morning, and Lacy sat slouched on a folding chair in the headquarters tent listening to Holcomb cuss out Matt Dunn.

The *alcalde* of the town had just left. Lacy had interpreted as the Mexican mayor presented a statement of charges for the damage done to the *calabozo* door, an amount that came from the major's own pocket, as had the fee for the army's use of the jail.

Lacy had trouble hiding his grin as the major raved on.

"The ornery sonofabitch could have walked through that door, if he'd just waited a bit," Holcomb raged. "What the hell did he have to burn it down for?"

"Don't reckon he knew it'd be opened for him, Major."

Holcomb calmed down slightly. "I suppose. Well, the less said about the whole thing, the better. But, by God! it gripes me to pay for something he deliberately set on fire."

"He took a hell of a chance," Lacy said. "It took guts to do what he did. He wanted out bad. Wanted to make sure he'd keep that showdown with Quintero."

A sly look came into the major's face. "Well, that's another charge I could put on him. Breaking out of confinement."

"If you'd dare call it that."

Holcomb met his yes coldly for a long moment, reading the accusation there. "Hell, I couldn't just release him officially," he said. "That'd be against regulations, the charges against him being what they are."

Lacy held back a grin and said, "You want me to take the Apaches and pick him up again?"

"Goddamit! No!"

CHAPTER 13

MAJOR Holcomb was not a regretful man.

Maybe he should have listened to Sergeant Dunn's warning back there in Gunlock about the nearness of the Villistas. But only a damn fool would put much stock in the information passed on by a local peon.

Maybe he had underestimated the intelligence of the Villista rear guard during the pursuit of the raiders after the attack.

And maybe he did misjudge the importance of this *macho* bull to that *federale* colonel when he tried to bluff him at Corrales.

He knew these were three blots on his service record.

But, by God, he now had his chance, and, with a little luck, he intended to wipe his record clean.

Holcomb had pleaded with Pershing, who had come down to Bachíniva to censure him for his rashness at Corrales, to let him strike toward Parral to find out where Villa was.

He had argued that his small command, only two troops of men, could move faster than any other and could hide where a larger force could not.

His aggressiveness had throughout Holcomb's career outweighed other blunders, and it finally won the general over; Pershing, frustrated in his mission to find Villa, reluctantly agreed. He did, however, order a Captain Stark, who had come down with him from Namiquipa, to accompany Holcomb as an observer.

Holcomb was glad to have Captain Stark with him, even though Stark was a mustanger, a man who had come up from the ranks of enlisted men. Major Holcomb actually knew Stark slightly. At San Juan, where Stark was a mere corporal in the platoon led by Second Lieutenant Holcomb, he had caught Holcomb's eye by his courageous conduct during the engagement. And in the Philippines, when Holcomb was a troop commander, Stark had been a field-commissioned lieutenant in one of the other troops of the same squadron.

Holcomb was elated to have Captain Stark along as observer, because Pershing had designated him Awards Officer of the Expedition.

That meant that Stark was there to look for brave action under fire, and Holcomb intended to show him just that. Two things were always in Holcomb's mind these days: the board of inquiry into his possible negligence at Gunlock and the possibility of getting himself promoted. A citation for a medal, signed and sworn to by the Awards Officer, could have great bearing on either of these.

The citation, of course, would have to be endorsed by Pershing, the Chief of Staff of the Army, and the Secretary of War. But, with luck, that could be routine.

The battles so far in the campaign had been few. And Holcomb was smart enough to guess that by now, in this bogged-down campaign, the top brass was hurting for stimulating news to feed the American public. Which was probably why they had a company-grade officer running around looking for heroes. There had been good action by the 7th Cavalry under Colonel Dodd at Guerrero at the end of March, with only five troopers wounded and fifty-six Villistas killed. Villa himself had taken a bullet there, it was rumored, the only time any American unit had made contact with him since the campaign began.

Until now.

And Dodd, who was sixty-three years old, had been cited
by Stark for the Silver Star and confirmed as a brigadier by
a grateful Senate. So far that was about all.

Well, what happened to Dodd could damn well happen
to Holcomb, he was thinking. And if Stark was looking for
another prospective recipient of a medal, Major Holcomb
was sure going to show him one.

Two days after Pershing's return to Namiquipa, Holcomb led his squadron out of Bachíniva. He rode at a slow
trot, and he kept this gait as long as the terrain permitted.

In two days he covered over eighty miles of the rugged
country north of Cusihuiriachi, a small town situated in a
canyon. A day after that he was in Cienégita and he turned
east, leaving the main road south to Parral. The next day he
was in Santa Rosalia de Cuevas and still moving fast. At
dawn he put the squadron south on a secondary route he
had picked from the map he carried.

In another two days the exhausted soldiers on their
fatigued horses reached Santa Cruz de Villegas, only thir-
teen miles from Parral but hidden from it by the mountainous terrain.

"Gentlemen," Holcomb said to his officers, "this is
where we will wait. Until the fifth day in May."

"That's a week away," Captain Walker said.

"Exactly," the major said.

The weather turned warm but not hot, and there was a
clear running stream with a fringe of *álamos* near the town.
It was a good spot for a bivouac.

Now that there was time, Captain Stark set about getting
acquainted with the officers of the squadron and trying to
learn the reason for Holcomb's halting there. He knew
Pershing had authorized a scouting mission as far south as
Parral.

Holcomb was closemouthed about this. In answer to
Stark's question he said, "I'm sending the civilian scout,

Lacy, into Parral to see what he can learn. In that vaquero outfit he wears and speaking Spanish the way he does, he can probably learn more from the Mexicans than we can riding around the country. And we'll keep the advantage of surprise."

That made sense, Stark had to admit. But little by little he began to piece together part of the picture. Lieutenant Darwin gave him a real clue. Stark had taken a liking to the young lieutenant during the ride down from Bachíniva. A couple of mornings after they arrived at Villegas he said, "I overheard some of the men talking about a Sergeant Dunn of your troop. He's a deserter?"

"Not to my way of thinking," Darwin said. He went on to tell Stark what had happened at Gunlock and after. He ended with "Captain, if you had seen him there with his wife dying in his arms, you could make a lot of allowance for what he's done."

"But Major Holcomb doesn't?"

"I'm afraid not, sir. Major Holcomb is strictly by-the-book. With enlisted men, at least."

The awards officer smiled faintly. "I wouldn't argue that point," he said. And although he had risen from sergeant's rank himself, or maybe *because* he had, he found himself feeling considerable sympathy for Dunn without even knowing him.

Lacy came back from Parral to make his first report to Holcomb. The major received it alone in his tent.

"What I find out is this, Major," Lacy said. "Dunn must have made the necessary connections in Parral, because the Mexican impresario who runs the bullfights is still promoting the gunfight. Damnedest thing I ever seen. You go in any cantina in that town and the first thing you see is a big printed poster advertising it for Cinco de Mayo."

"Posters?"

"Just like a bullfight cartel. CAPITÁN RODOLFO QUINTERO Y SARGENTO GRINGO! MANO A MANO!"

"Sergeant *Gringo?*"

"That's what the Mexicans have taken to calling him. And from what I gather, he's got a lot of sympathy for his side. Quintero, it appears, ain't especially well liked by most of the Mexicans in Parral, even though they are supposed to be Villa sympathizers."

"What about Villa? Is he going to be there?"

"He's expected."

"With how many men?"

"A small bodyguard of his elite Dorados, the way I hear it. Most of his men have gone back to their homes, at least until he gets active again. Won't have no more than a dozen, most likely. Of course, all I know is hearsay."

"Any of those goddam *federales* around?" Holcomb said.

"None anybody knows about. Nearest known are those up north at Corrales."

Holcomb said, "I don't want you telling anybody else about this. Nobody. And that includes Captain Stark."

"Sure, Major. You want me to go back to Parral now and hang around some more? It's five days yet till the *duelo.*"

"Might be better if you stay here a couple of days, then go in for a last-minute intelligence gather. You hang around those cantinas too much, some of those Mexicans might get suspicious."

"All right, Major." Lacy hesitated. "You mentioned Captain Stark. I been wondering what his job is."

Holcomb said, "He's the awards officer for the campaign."

"What does that mean?"

"He's free to move around wherever he thinks there might be interesting action. His duty is to write citations for any officers or men who deserve recognition."

Lacy said, "You mean write them up for being brave or smart in battle—and like that?"

"That's the gist of it."

"Don't reckon he's been getting much writer's cramp lately," Lacy said.

"Maybe we can change that."

"Kind of figured you was working on it," Lacy said.

He left the tent and was followed by Stark, who had been waiting a few yards away. Stark caught up to him near the enlisted men's tents. "Hold on, Lacy."

The scout stopped, saw Stark, and his face took on a wary look.

The awards officer smiled faintly, guessing that Holcomb had warned him to give out nothing. "Been to Parral, Lacy?"

"Can't say."

"Any news of Villa?"

"Can't say."

"What about Sergeant Dunn?"

"What about him?"

"Where is he?"

"Can't say."

Stark grinned at him. "Lacy, I've just broken your code."

"Broken my what?"

"Broken your code."

"I never knew I had one, Captain."

"Every time you answer 'Can't say,' you must mean yes. Otherwise you'd say 'No.' Right?"

"Can't—"

"So you've been to Parral. You have news about Villa. And you know where Sergeant Dunn is."

Lacy gave him a sullen look. "I didn't tell you none of that."

Stark said amiably, "No, you didn't. You're doing your job well."

"Put me in for a medal, then," Lacy said and walked away.

It had given Stark something to think about. He thought

about it as he made his way to the major's tent. He spoke to the orderly standing nearby, and Holcomb overheard him.

The major lifted the flap and said, "Come in, Stark, come in."

Stark was used to this affected heartiness toward him by superior officers. After all, a citation by him could mean a lot to an officer's future career. But he didn't think he had yet let this special treatment influence his judgment.

Now he said, "Major, what the hell is going on?"

"What do you mean? I'm waiting here while I have Lacy scout out the situation around Parral."

"The way you force-marched us down here from Bachíniva, I thought you had something more definite in mind."

"Don't be impatient. You'll see some action."

"When?"

Holcomb did not answer specifically. "Soon," he said.

Stark studied the squadron commander thoughtfully. Holcomb had always been a puzzle. In Cuba, in the Philippines, and now in Mexico. He said, "I hope to see some. An awards officer in a stalled campaign is about as useful as teats on a bull." He paused. "It is not a duty I particularly like. I'd rather have my command back."

Holcomb said, "I've not asked before, but what led to your appointment?"

Stark shrugged. "Who knows? I had command of a troop at Fort Bliss, and then the raids came and I had new orders. I think Pershing chose me himself."

"I recall that your combat record was good," Holcomb said.

"Good enough, I guess. As was yours." Stark's face took on a distant look. "Man, talk about action—that morning in the Philippines on Jolo Island when we went up the slopes of Mount Bagsak to hit the Moro stronghold!"

"It was hell getting up through that jungle growth," the major said, "I remember that. Though it hid us for a while from their guns."

"It didn't hide us from the machetes and the *bolo* knives and those broad-bladed *barongs* and the spears they threw at us," Stark recalled.

"I know," the major said. "One of the bastards laid my guts open with a *bolo* while I was sticking a dead private's bayonet into his."

"And Pershing was right there in the thick of it," Stark remembered. "I saw him myself during the last hours near the top. Standing there giving orders and ignoring the weapons thrown at him."

"He could have had the Medal of Honor."

"He could have," Stark said. "I was one of those who got the testimonials and affidavits together to send to the adjutant general. But Pershing turned the medal down. Said he was only doing his duty, standing there on that mountain. He finally accepted the Distinguished Service Medal instead."

Holcomb said, "That might have been why he chose you as awards officer here."

Stark shrugged. "Could be. If so, he certainly didn't do me any favor."

The major was thoughtful. He said, "Cheer up. You may have something to write about very shortly."

"Stop being vague, Major. Give me some details."

"What do you want to know?"

"I've been picking up a little here, a little there. Just where does this Sergeant Dunn fit into the picture?"

"How do you know he does?"

"I'm guessing. If I'm wrong, tell me."

Holcomb was momentarily ruffled by the captain's brusque tone, but he hid it quickly. "All right," he said resignedly. "Dunn fits in. He's the key figure in this."

"A deserter?"

"That's right. But if things work out, he could be instrumental in putting Villa right into my hands."

"Why are we waiting here?"

"I've got to wait for this Mexican holiday coming up."

Stark thought for a moment. "Cinco de Mayo?"

"Yeah. That one."

"Why?"

Holcomb took a deep breath. "I'll give you the whole story. Then get off my back with your damn questions."

"Let's have it."

Again Holcomb was irritated, but he said, "You ever see a bullfight?"

"A couple. When I was at Bliss I went over to Juárez a time or two to see them. Believe me, those matadors got guts to spare, my way of thinking." He paused. "There's going to be a bullfight in Parral?"

"Not exactly," Holcomb said. "But something just as gutsy." He grinned. "You aren't going to believe this, but here it is anyway." He laid it out for Stark, about Sergeant Dunn and Quintero and, hopefully, Villa too.

When he finished he looked for Stark's reaction. But the captain just shook his head a couple of times in silence. Then he got right to the point. "So what is your plan of action?"

"I figured you'd be a little more surprised than you appear to be," Holcomb said.

"I'm dumbfounded. What are you going to do?"

"I'll move the squadron into Parral just before four o'clock on the afternoon of the fifth. I figure most of the damn town will be at the arena to see the gunfight. At four we'll move on the arena and grab Villa."

"He'll be alone?"

"He'll have a few bodyguards. Nothing to worry about."

"Why take him alive?" Stark said. Then before Holcomb

could answer, he said, "You don't need to tell me that. I know. If you can take him alive you can get your picture in every newspaper in the world, posing beside him as his captor. The benefits of that are easy enough to see. Hell, Major, you might be made a brigadier general over the heads of eight, nine hundred senior officers."

Holcomb scowled. "Don't get sarcastic."

"I'm not. I'm just stating a possibility."

Holcomb continued to scowl. "The thought never entered my mind," he said.

On the afternoon of May 4 an exhausted dispatch rider arrived at the squadron encampment and was brought to Major Holcomb's tent.

The major heard the commotion of his arrival and went outside. The rider saluted, making a great effort to stand erect.

"Major Holcomb?"

Holcomb nodded.

"Private Rutledge, sir. I have a dispatch from Namiquipa."

"From Namiquipa? A long ride."

"Been five days on the road, sir."

Holcomb took the sealed envelope the messenger had pulled from a pocket. He said to an orderly, "See that this man is fed and that his horse is taken care of."

"Yes, sir."

Captain Stark's small tent was pitched nearby, and he had been lounging in front of it. Now he got up and came over to Holcomb and said, "Must be urgent to make him ride that hard."

The major showed concern. "Goddamit! Tomorrow we hit Parral. I hate to open this thing."

"No choice, is there, Major?"

Holcomb ripped open the envelope and unfolded a paper. "It's a general order from headquarters. Dated 29

April." He began to read and then he began to swear.

Stark waited, saying nothing. Holcomb finished reading, looked at him, then shoved the dispatch out to him. "Here! You read it for yourself."

Stark read, his eyes skipping over it:

> To all field commanders. . . . Troops of all provisional squadrons of the Expedition will be reassembled immediately under their own regimental guidons. . . . Each regiment will be assigned a district of Chihuahua from which strikes against Villistas can be made if such opportunities present themselves. . . . However, due to strenuous objection by the Carranza government to our State Department, any probes further south into Mexico are not to be undertaken. . . . The following is to be the immediate redeployment of the cavalry regiments: 7th Cavalry to Guerrero; 10th Cavalry to Headquarters at Namiquipa; 13th Cavalry to Lake Bustillos; 5th Cavalry to Satevó; and 11th Cavalry to San Francisco de Borja. . . . The provisional squadrons of the Expedition will be reassembled immediately under their own regimental guidons. . . . Each regiment will be assigned a district of Chihuahua from eral.

"Well?" the major said.

"It's plain enough," Stark said. "Rotten luck."

Holcomb said nothing. He refolded the order and shoved it into the flap pocket of his shirt.

"Kind of spoils the fun, doesn't it, Major?"

Holcomb still didn't answer.

Stark gave him a hard look. "You aren't thinking of something rash?"

"What would you do?"

"Pull out for Satevó, of course," Stark said. "You're to join the 5th there."

"I thought you wanted to see some action," Holcomb said.

Stark stared at him. Finally he said, "Major, I have heard men refer to you as Old Guts-for-brains. I'm beginning to see why."

"I asked if you still wanted to see action," Holcomb said shortly.

Stark took a long time to answer. Then he nodded. "As long as it is your decision. And for the record, you didn't show me that general order."

Holcomb grinned. "I'll show it to you tomorrow night. After the ball is over."

Stark shook his head. "No. I just changed my mind. I might be asked under oath if I saw it before the action. So I've seen it, and for the record I protest your intention to strike at Parral."

"All right, Captain. You've gone on record with your protest. Now let's get on with the preparations for tomorrow."

CHAPTER 14

THE bells of the Church of the Virgin of the Thunderbolt awakened Matt. They were answered by the bells from Our Lady of Fatima. He awoke in Juanita's room with his nerves already taut. Sunlight blazed through a window whose shutters she had opened, reminding him that the final day had come.

He looked at the battered clock on the small table beside the bed. It was just past eight. He had slept late after a restless night in which he'd once seen Molly's face calling to him from a ring of orange flames, calling for him to kill Quintero for what he had done.

Just past eight. Eight hours from now it would all be over, one way or the other. At four o'clock in the afternoon of the fifth of May in the year of 1916. He stared at the ceiling, feeling a knot grow in his stomach.

The outside door opened and Juanita came in with a tray. He could smell a breakfast of tortillas and eggs fried with chilis.

"From the cantina," she said. "Rafael fixed it for you. I let you sleep because you tossed much during the night."

"Yes," he said.

She went to the window and opened it, letting in the morning air and the sounds of the people of Parral moving around getting ready for the celebration of Cinco de Mayo.

He felt the excitement outside as much as he heard it. A festive, expectant, eager buzz ran through the crowd. They are eager to see the *duelo*, he thought. I have made their

day for them. I have added something extra to their holiday.

"The breakfast will get cold," she said.

"I have no hunger. But when you go back to the cantina,
thank Gómez for me."

"I will not go back, not today."

"Is he here, have you heard?"

She shrugged. "Nobody seems to know yet. But he will
be here, of course."

"Of course."

"Nobody has ever questioned Quintero's courage."

"Then, too, there will be Villa forcing him," he said.

"He will need no forcing," she said. "Believe me." She
looked at him and came close and put her arms around him
and pressed her cheek against his chest. "Ah, Mateo! I
pray that you beat him!"

There was a knock at the door. She went out of the bedroom to answer it, and he heard a man's voice. He heard
her say *Gracias*," and then shut the door.

She came back to where he was. "He is here," she said.
"A neighbor brought news. He has been seen riding in
with Villa and a few of Villa's Dorados."

"All right," he said. "There is nothing to worry about,
then."

She looked at him oddly. "You are loco, Mateo. Do you
know that?"

"Maybe."

"Try to eat something."

"All right."

She took the tray, carried it to the other room, and placed
it on the small dining table. He followed her, seated himself, and began picking at the food.

There was another rap at the door. She opened it a crack,
then more widely and stepped back as Luis Beltrán, the
impresario of the bullring, came in.

"*Hola, Señor Sargento*," Beltrán said. "Is all in order?"

"*Creo que sí.*"

"Good. I stopped by to check and to tell you that Quintero is ready. Villa has come to watch. And it appears we will have a capacity crowd."

Matt looked at him curiously. Beltrán appeared in great spirits. He wondered how much the impresario was charging for admission. It was something he had not thought about.

Beltrán caught his look and interpreted its meaning. "There is something I did not mention before," he said, smiling. "A matter of money. There are expenses, of course, the conditioning of the arena in this, the off season, and the printing of tickets and—"

"Tickets?" Matt said.

"—Of course. And advertising: word was spread around by hired voices and some posters were clandestinely placed in various cantinas and. . . ." His voice trailed off and his smile faded under Matt's stare.

"Go on," Matt said.

Beltrán cleared his throat. He was a chunky man, with dark skin, and looked to Matt like a million other Mexicans, except that he was wearing an American-style suit that must have cost a month's pay for a dozen peons. He went on: "Well, as I was saying, there have been expenses. But nothing like those of a corrida. For one thing, I did not have to buy bulls. For another, I do not have to pay matadors. Well, of course, you are the matadors. You are the killers, no?" He gave a slight laugh. His smile came back.

"So, Sergeant Gringo, I have decided you should share in the receipts. That's only fair, is it not? Ten percent of the gate receipts. What do you think of that?"

"Generous," Matt said. He picked up a tortilla, bit into it, and began to chew.

"Of course," Luis Beltrán said, "it would be a matter of winner take all. The loser will have little use for money, *verdad?*" He chuckled again.

"*Verdad,*" Matt said. He dug into some of the eggs and chili. With his mouth full he said, "There is, though, the matter of a funeral."

"Of course," Beltrán said. "I will take care of that expense. I am not unfeeling."

"You are a generous man, Señor Impresario. And I appreciate your giving me this opportunity to display my skills as a matador."

The impresario laughed. "Truly you have courage, gringo. To joke at a time like this!"

"I am too big to cry."

"Yes. Well, I must get back to the arena. A hundred details to watch out for. Until later, then."

"Until four *de la tarde.*"

"At least a few minutes before, please!" Beltrán said. "Please do not be late. You have no idea what a strain a *duelo* like this puts on a man."

Juanita ushered him out and closed the door. She looked at Matt. "Are we all crazy?" she said.

Hunger had come to him, and he finished the breakfast. He stood up and a nervous restlessness took him, so that he could not stay still. He began to pace back and forth across the room. Juanita eyed him curiously but made no comment.

When he couldn't stand the crampedness of the quarters any longer, he grabbed the door and flung it open. On the street in front of the place a crowd was standing vigil.

One of the crowd called, "*Hola!* Sergeant Gringo." And another called, "That you have luck in this afternoon!"

He stared at them for a moment and then his eyes fell and he said to himself, "Jesus Christ!"

That's when he saw the rose-colored envelope lying on the step in front of the door. He could see his name handwritten on the face of it. My name? he thought. Well, not exactly. The words, in feminine flourish, *Sargento Gringo.* He picked the envelope up and he could smell the cheap perfume from waist height.

Some of the crowd saw him pick it up, and possibly they had seen it placed there and were awaiting his reaction. He was aware of this, and he gave them a show—he raised it to his nostrils and inhaled deeply. There was laughter from the crowd. One of them shouted, "*Sargento!* Already you are lucky!"

He held the envelope high and waved it, then stepped back and closed the door. "There's a crowd out there," he said.

Juanita said, "What is that in your hand?"

Before he could answer she'd reached him and snatched it from his grasp. She wrinkled her nose. "It stinks like a privy," she said. She tore it open and ripped from it a single sheet of matching paper.

"Let me read it," he said.

"No! Can you read Spanish?" Her eyes were flicking over the message and becoming slits.

"Goddamit! Read it to me, then."

"You want to know what it says? All right. Listen to this stupid whore, this *puta estupida!*"

"Read it."

" '*Mi querido Sargento Gringo*,'—oh, the stupid whore! —'if luck favors you this afternoon and you wish to celebrate your triumph afterward with the favors of a passionate woman, I will be outside the Cantina Vargas on Calle Gabino Barreda from seven this evening. You will know me because I am that rarity—a handsome Mexican girl who has real blond hair. Signed, La Rubia.' "

"Now I've got to win," he said.

"*Rubia!*" she said. "Real blond hair, my *culo!* Real out of a *botella* of peroxide! *Qúe puta chingada!*"

There was another knock on the door.

"Is there some other place we can go, Juanita? I mean, to wait through the day?"

"*Sí*, Mateo."

The knock was repeated, louder this time. She opened the door only the width of her face and peered out. He could hear her remonstrating with someone, then she voiced a loud "No!" and shut the door hard.

"That was . . . ?"

"The parish priest. Asking if you had given thought to willing to the church, if you lose, the money you might have coming from the receipts at the arena."

"What did you tell him?"

"That you spend your money on peroxide blonds."

"Jesus Christ! Let's get out of here."

"First you must dress properly for the *duelo*. Because we will not be coming back here."

"I am dressed."

"But not properly."

"What do you want me to do? Put on a bullfighter's 'suit of lights'?"

"No," she said, "this." She went into the bedroom and came back with his cavalry uniform, with its sleeves showing where the sergeant's stripes had been ripped off. "This is your suit of lights. This is what you wore when it all began. This is what you must wear when it ends. Be proud of it, gringo. Wear it proudly this afternoon in front of us all." Then she said, "I am sorry it is wrinkled. I carried it from Cobán in my saddlebag. I have fitted my gun and holster to fit your army belt also." She held that up too so he could see it. "That cavalry holster with the flap was not made for gun duels."

When he was dressed and ready, he said, "How do we leave without that crowd following?"

"Let them follow."

"Let them follow?"

"To Gómez's place. We will enter and walk right through and out the back service door. I will take you then to a place away from disturbance."

Their destination was a short walk out of town, part of an abandoned old mine complex. There was a short climb up and then they rested under a wood portico, which fronted a crude building.

"I discovered this place long ago," she said. "I come

here sometimes alone to look down on the town. It was once a mine superintendent's quarters, I think. This was a gringo mining venture that failed. Did you see the company signs forbidding trespass as we climbed up? I ignore them."

"A crude place to come," Matt said. He looked about him at the bleak cluster of shacks and rusted equipment and piles of ore slag. "Couldn't you find a prettier place?"

"I have never come here seeking beauty," Juanita said. "You must understand what it is to be a cantina girl, Mateo. Tolerated by men because of my sex, but despised by other women for that very reason. Looked down upon by nearly all. Well, I come here when I want to look down on them! Look down on their ugly town and their ugly, grubbing lives. We fought for them, Mateo, you and I, but did it help? Six years and things are right back where they were before. Was the killing worth this?"

"I don't know," he said.

"Will the killing this afternoon, if it is you—" She broke off, struggling for words. "Will it be worth it?"

He looked out over the town, at the mountains all around, but he did not see them. "It has to be done," he said.

The Virgin of the Thunderbolt's bells sounded the hour of three. "It is time to go down," Juanita said.

He had been lying with his head in her lap, staring at the sky. He got to his feet. "All right," he said.

The street leading to the bullring was thronged with people. They walked in silence toward the shadow of the big curved wall, with the noise and the movement growing around them. Matt could hear a band playing. People were pushing toward the plaza, anxious to get good seats. Several, attracted by his uniform, stared, then, recognizing him, called out, "Olé! Sergeant Gringo." Others simply stared in awe.

He could feel their excitement and their tension as his own.

Three Dorados rode up and stopped him. They had guns

pointed at him before he realized they were anything but charros in for the festival. One of them said, "Do nothing foolish, gringo. We are acting on Villa's orders."

"What do you want?"

"We are taking the girl. She has been invited to sit beside *el general* to watch the *duelo.*"

"Why?"

"It is the desire of *el general.*"

Juanita said, "It is all right, Mateo. I am not afraid."

"But why?" Matt said again.

The Dorado said, "Insurance for the general, *sargento.* Any sign of a trap, any treachery, and she takes a bullet through her pretty head. You understand? Villa has given you your chance at vengeance. He trusts you to an unusual degree. But me, I am not so sure. So remember this: If there is trouble I will kill her."

Luis Beltrán stepped out of his office on the patio under the stands. *"Por Dios!"* he said. "You had me worried. And I did not need more of that! Not an hour ago a bull I have been holding for a future corrida broke open the corral gate and was smashing the wood of the runway. We just now got him locked up — temporarily — in the *toril,* the holding pen."

There was a passageway that led from the patio farther under the stands and beyond a gate into the ring. Matt could see through the tunnel it formed to where the sunlight shone on the empty sand of the ring, and to the stands on the other side, where he saw the crowds filling their seats.

Beltrán took a silk handkerchief from his pocket and wiped his forehead. "Yes, maestro, you, too, gave me a scare, thinking you—well, thinking you might have forgotten and—"

"Is Quintero here?"

"Yes, señor. He is in the chapel where the *toreros* make their devotions before a corrida." Beltrán pointed across the patio to the elaborate front of a tiny chapel, next to the near end of the passageway. "May I beg that you wait until he comes out before you enter to make your own?"

"I do not pray," Matt said. "Not for luck in killing another man."

"Yes, of course. I was forgetting you are gringo," Beltrán said. He mopped again at his face with his handkerchief and exhaled strongly. There was the smell of tequila on his breath. "I will tell you this," he said. "There is a great strain on a man promoting a venture like this."

"I feel for you," Matt said. "But I can only guess at how you are suffering."

"I appreciate your sympathy, señor," the impresario said. He took out a stem-winding watch from his vest pocket. "A quarter to four," he said. "When Captain Quintero comes from the chapel, I must explain the details of this *faena* to you both. You will find the rules simple and—" He broke off as a short, oxlike figure came running across the patio.

"Gómez!" Matt said. "*Qué pasó?*"

The *cantinero* was out of breath but he did not stop to catch it. "Thank God! Mateo, I caught you. A thing has happened — there is an American major with a troop of cavalry—no matter how I learned this—from customers of my cantina, of course — but this *chingao* major has deployed a force around Parral ready and waiting to crash in and capture Villa and—"

"When?"

Gómez shrugged. "When all are intent on the *duelo*, how else?"

Beltrán seemed not to be listening. His eyes were on the door to the chapel. He pulled out his watch again. "It lacks ten minutes," he said. "And there is Qunitero finished with his devotions. Come, *sargento!* It is time to begin." He took Matt by the arm and started toward the passageway to the arena.

"Mateo!" Gómez said. "What about the gringo major?"

"I don't know," Matt said. His eyes were on Quintero

waiting for them by the tunnel. But only half his mind was there. The rest was on the warning of Villa's Dorado. *"Any sign of a trap . . . and she takes a bullet through her pretty head."*

He and Quintero met at the head of the passageway; their eyes sought each other's gaze and held, staring.

Beltrán shorter than either, found himself between them, and sweat broke out again on his round face, a muscle began to twitch in his cheek. He looked from one to the other and said in a nervous rush of words, "You have met before, eh, señores? So there is not the need to introduce you. Please follow me into the arena and there I will give you the final instructions. Señores, if you will follow me." He moved jerkily down the passageway, as if his knees weren't quite able to support him.

Matt and Quintero followed, neither now looking at the other. Their eyes were straight ahead and fixed on the glare of the arena at the end of the tunnel.

The impresario reached the end and stopped. He stood in the last of the shade before the arena and again he wiped his face. He looked quickly at Matt and then at Quintero. His eyes fell and he could not look at either of them again. Mother of God! he thought. They both wear masks instead of faces. What kind of men are these? What are their thoughts? A shudder ran through him and he said shakily, "Señores, please step now into the arena."

The crowd saw them and broke into a roar. The band struck up the opening drumbeats of "La Virgen de la Macarena."

Beltrán jerked out his watch and almost dropped it. "It lacks two minutes," he said, but the dryness of his throat made his words inaudible even to himself.

He coughed and forced himself to speak louder, and the words came out unevenly. "Señores, please listen to me. The rules have been set by General Villa himself. You have heard them, but I will repeat them.

"You are each to walk slowly along the curve of the *bar-*

rera, the fence, until you are at opposite sides of the arena. You can see your spots marked on the *barrera* with a white flag on the one side and a black flag on the other.

"You will see that the positions have been selected so that neither of you will have the sun in his eyes. Also that the seats behind each position are empty—they have been roped off from the spectators. Thus, unless there is a very wild shot, there will be no danger to them."

He reached into his coat pocket and took out a metal disk. "I will toss this disk with your names stenciled on either side. The one whose name comes up will have his choice of the white or the black position. You agree?"

When neither commented, Beltrán went on: "You will now check your pistols. Since you both carry the Colt .45 revolver, you will have six shots in full cylinder." He looked at their waists, seeing the ammo pouches on Matt's web belt and the cartridge belt worn guerrilla-style by Quintero. "And you have extra shells—if they are needed."

Both Matt and Quintero broke open their guns and checked the loads one last time. The band had stopped playing and the crowd, seeing the men check their weapons, broke out in another roar.

"And now, señores," the impresario said and tossed the disk into the air, and it fell to the sand.

Matt looked down and saw the single word *Gringo.* "The white," he said.

"Señores," Beltrán said, "when you reach your positions, you may fire at will."

They turned and each began walking along the *barrera* toward his flag.

Matt reached the white flag and faced across the arena. Quintero was there, waiting.

CHAPTER 15

IT was the moment of truth, Matt thought, and his mind wasn't where it ought to be. His mind was on Juanita in a box with Villa, and on the Dorado with a pistol to her head if there was a trap, and on Major Holcomb and the 12th Cavalry poised to spring one.

I lost one woman, he thought, Now I'm going to lose another. So she's a cantina girl. A cantina girl, you silly bastard. Don't think about her. Think about Quintero.

A bullet slammed through the *barrera* beside him and smacked against the concrete wall behind it.

The sound snapped him into action. Quintero was going to kill him. The Dorado was going to kill Juanita. All for nothing. He couldn't let her die for nothing. He couldn't let Molly die for nothing, either.

He charged madly toward Quintero, heedless of two quick shots he heard from Quintero's gun but did not feel. He fired coldly as he ran, raising his gun and sighting it against Quintero. His bullet kicked sand at Quintero's feet. El Matador, they called Quintero, eh? Well he, Sergeant Gringo, was the bull in this *faena*.

He heard the scream of the crowd as they recognized this. I am the bull! he shouted to himself. He fired again and saw the red blotch gush through Quintero's jacket.

You've taken the horn, Matador! *My* horn, you raping, murdering bastard! He fired again, still plunging, and saw the blood spurt from Quintero's belly. Smoke belched from

Qunitero's gun and a shot stabbed his own shoulder. Oh ho, Matador! Your sword isn't accurate, you missed the lung, you missed the heart!

His next shot missed.

He fired again, close now, and the slug smashed into Quintero's rib cage and spun him hard against the *barrera* and Quintero fell.

He reached Quintero, raging and wild, and far off he could hear the insane screaming of the crowd, and Quintero tried to lift his gun.

He reached down and shoved the muzzle of his gun against Quintero's head. And hesitated.

For a moment he stood there, motionless and panting, while the crowd screamed for him to give the coup de grace.

He couldn't bring himself to do it. And then Quintero's gun fell from his hand and he rolled back with his eyes staring empty at the sky.

Some lunatic in the stands yelled, *"Olé!"*

The insanity of the cry dispelled his own. Juanita! He had to reach Juanita.

He jerked his eyes to the box above his head and saw her there, on her feet with the rest, beside Villa and his bodyguards and the Dorado who had taken her from him.

She was safe—alive! But his relief was gone in a second.

Outside the stadium he could hear the shooting begin. Above the screaming of the crowd he heard the crack of the Springfields. Holcomb had attacked.

And he saw the Dorado up in the box pull out his gun and put it to Juanita's head.

CHAPTER 16

MAJOR Holcomb had moved his troops up quietly to within two hundred yards of the bullring. He held them there, dismounted, their mounts given over to the horse holders. He waited, listening to the crowd roar and the band begin to sound "La Macarena."

Captain Stark, standing beside him, said, "Just when do you close in, Major?"

Holcomb said, "When we hear the pistol shots of the duel. According to Lacy, there are only a half-dozen bodyguards in there with Villa."

A minute went by, and another, and then suddenly the gunshots sounded from inside the arena.

"Forward—ho!" Holcomb shouted and led the charge for the entrance plaza to the stadium.

And a hundred hidden Dorados opened fire from slits in the adjacent adobe bull corral where the bulls were kept when there was to be a corrida.

As the bodyguard lifted his gun to Juanita's head Matt acted without thought, but knowing there was only one bullet left in his gun and glad he had not used it in a coup de grace on Quintero. He raised the Colt and aimed fast and pulled the trigger and hoped to God he was lucky.

He was. He saw the bodyguard's forehead burst into a red blossom, his big hat flying loose, and then the man was gone from sight at the feet of the others.

Juanita saw Matt and moved. She came leaping like a jaguar to the top of the concrete wall and then dropped its ten feet into the sand of the *callejón,* the narrow alleyway between the concrete wall and the wood *barrera,* landing in a heap. He jumped the *barrera* and pulled her against the wall out of the line of fire of other shots he heard whining in ricochet off the top of it.

The wild shots ceased, and Matt guessed Villa and his guards were shoving their way out of the stands to reach the combat, which seemed to be outside or just underneath the stands.

"Mateo! Oh God! Mateo. You did it!"

He reached down and pulled her to her feet. "Are you hurt?"

"No. *Soy como gata.* I am like a cat. But are we safe here?"

The answer came before he could give it. It came as the thunder of a gun crashing in the *callejón* and in the sight of a brown hand lowered over the wall pointing the gun in their direction.

The gun thundered again, and he grabbed her hand and ducked out through the *burladero* opening into the arena. He crouched low and pulled her along the blind side of the fence, racing for the main entry.

He could hear the boards of the *barrera* splintering as four spaced shots shattered the wood, each striking just behind them. And then they were out of the arena and into the passage exit and running through the cool air of the tunnel.

The first volley from the Dorados had knocked down a dozen troopers. The others turned in the direction of the fire and charged the slitted adobe wall. More intense fire drove them back.

Holcomb, in the front of it, was driven back with the rest. Miraculously, he was not hit.

Matt, coming from the passage with Juanita at his heels, looked beyond the entrance plaza and saw it all at a glance. His first impulse was to rush forward to join the troopers, to show that damn major whose side he was on.

He changed his mind fast. He'd get himself killed quick, and probably Juanita too.

He said to her, "Run for the chapel! Stay inside until this is over." He grabbed her and gave her a shove and saw her running across the patio. She reached the ornate door, tugged it open, and slipped inside, and he breathed again.

He turned then and ran back through the passage to the arena. Above him the panicked, bewildered crowd was surging one way and then another. People fell down and were trampled upon, men shouted and women screamed.

He glanced up only once and saw that Villa and his bodyguards were not in sight. He broke into the open and headed for the *toril's* red gate, through which the bulls were released for a *faena*.

The gate was locked, and he jumped to catch its top with his fingers and felt the sharp agony of the wound from Quintero's bullet. Still he managed to hang on, and he swung his leg up, got over somehow, and dropped to the other side.

His plan was vaguely formed in his mind. He was trying to work his way around behind the Dorados. If he attacked from there—it was a long shot, but it might give the troopers a chance to breach the walls of the bull corral, slip through its narrow slits, and close in to smother the deadly fire from there.

The bull came out of nowhere and its lunge missed him by an inch, its black-tipped horns thudding into the wood beside him.

He scrambled to the top of the chute gate, shaking with fright. "Goddam!" he said aloud, and then he remembered Beltrán's telling him about the bull.

He looked down at that ton of blackness snorting below

him and kicking dirt. Then it flung high its huge head, red eyes staring at him, arched neck swollen with bunched shoulder muscles, and he could have sworn it was breathing fire.

His vague plan came into focus.

He dropped outside the pen on the side toward the corral, reached down, and pulled up on the chute gate. He heard the bull grunt. Then, with nostrils flaring, it plunged out of the holding cage and rushed snorting down the runway. It struck the broken gate, flung it aside, and charged into the corral and straight for the fighting Dorados.

One of them sensed the thudding hooves behind him and started to turn and took a horn through his buttock. The bull tossed its head and the Dorado came loose, screaming from the impaling point, and sailed high and over the wall of the corral.

The others heard his scream and then the bull was among them, hooking and goring and tossing. They fired wildly, panicked, shouted, trying to escape the terrible horns.

Some turned and ran toward the south side of the bull corral, wanting to reach the horse corral, where they had left their mounts.

The bull charged after them and caught a straggler.

Some went out through the slits on the east side and were cut down by fire from Holcomb's cavalry.

In two minutes the tide of the battle had changed. Troopers poured in through the slits, shooting and swinging and clubbing, and the Dorados broke and ran, then saw the bull ahead of them and stopped to make a stand. At the south end of the corral somebody finally killed the rampaging animal.

The Dorados bunched nearest to where Matt now crouched by the broken runway gate and turned back on the troopers, some of whom were trying to reload their weapons.

A Dorado took a cigar from his mouth, lit the fuse of a homemade grenade, and threw the grenade among them.

Matt saw it land. He dived for it, grabbed it up as the sparks from the sputtering fuse touched his hand, and heaved it back into the Dorados' midst.

The explosion was deafening. It struck the adobe walls and bounced back, and then, above the ringing in his ears, he heard the cries and moans of the Villistas.

The survivors withdrew through the south end's wall slits, exchanging fire with the troopers as they backed away. Once beyond the wall they fled to their horses.

Matt was with the troopers chasing after them now, his uniform just another among the many. He reached a slit and went through and saw the Villistas leaping for their saddles. Those already mounted were driving their spurs in and racing away down the road to Durango.

Matt spotted among them, and not a hundred feet away, the chunky broad back of Pancho Villa. He raised his gun and sighted it between Villa's shoulders.

At that moment Villa turned in his saddle to look back, and Matt could swear he was grinning at him.

Matt let his gun arm drop. Ah, hell! he thought, *he* gave me my chance at Quintero.

Night had come. The fires were lit and the blankets of the wounded men being tended by the medics were strewn all over the field.

"Not the best of scenes, Major," Stark said.

Holcomb scowled. "Villa took the brunt of the casualties, Stark. At least three to one."

"And Villa got away."

"I came close. Damn close. Closer than anybody else in this damn campaign."

"Granted," Captain Stark said.

Holcomb's scowl faded. He looked at Stark. "I take it, then, you consider the action a success."

"Not a success, Major. But a bold and enterprising attempt to achieve the goal of the expedition. Bad luck, Villa getting away. You might have ended the campaign in one stroke here. As you said, you came closer than anybody to date. And did it on your own initiative. 'Meritorious and distinguished service in a position of great responsibility' is what the Service Medal is awarded for. And that's the way I'll put it when I write up the citation for you."

"Service Medal," Holcomb said, and he couldn't quite hide the elation in his voice. "Well, I appreciate that, Stark."

"There is just one other thing, Major."

Holcomb looked at him warily.

"There is the case of Sergeant Dunn," the captain said. "I personally witnessed some of what he did this afternoon. And I've been talking to men who witnessed the rest. Do you realize, Major, that he quite possibly saved you from disaster?"

The major looked unhappy. "Dunn?" he said.

"Furthermore, if he hadn't engaged in this gunfight with Quintero, you would never have had the opportunity to attempt the action you did. In other words, Major, without Dunn you would have achieved nothing. Don't you agree?"

"I'm not certain that—"

"I am," Stark said. He took from his shirt pocket a notebook and opened it to a page on which he had scribbled in pencil. He began to read aloud:

" 'Matthew Dunn, Sergeant, D Troop, 12th Cavalry, for extraordinary heroism in action. On 5 May 1916, at plus 1600 hours, during an attack by a provisional squadron of his regiment on an elite force of enemy Villistas. . . .' " Stark looked up and closed the notebook. "I'm citing him for the Distinguished Service Cross."

"Sergeant Dunn?" Major Holcomb said in a dead voice.

"And Major, this is an award I want to see go through.

The man deserves it, and I'm going to do my damnedest to see he gets it."

Holcomb got life back in his voice. "The man is under charges, Stark, serious charges. I don't see how—"

"So the charges will have to be dropped, won't they? We've got ourselves a hero here, Major. One who, possibly, earned *you* a medal. We can't see him brought up on charges, can we? That would spoil the whole thing."

Holcomb lost his voice again. He tried to speak but couldn't.

Finally he got the words out. "No," he said. "I guess we can't."

Juanita found Matt where he lay on his blankets among the other wounded. She kissed him and then her fingers caressed his bandaged shoulder where Quintero's slug had ripped the flesh.

"Ay, Mateo," she said sadly, "now it is the shoulder that keeps me from your embrace. That someday I should have you when you are not suffering from a hurt. I pray it!"

He grinned. "That it may be soon," he said.

If you have enjoyed this book and would like to receive
details of other Walker Western titles, please write to:

Western Editor
Walker and Company
720 Fifth Avenue
New York, NY 10019